Summer in the City

Summer in the City

BY *Marie-Louise Gay*
AND *David Homel*

GROUNDWOOD BOOKS
HOUSE OF ANANSI PRESS
TORONTO   BERKELEY

The authors would like to thank Shelley Tanaka for
her work as their editor.

Text copyright © 2012 by David Homel and Marie-Louise Gay
Illustrations copyright © 2012 by Marie-Louise Gay
Published in Canada and the USA in 2012 by Groundwood Books

Groundwood Books / House of Anansi Press
110 Spadina Avenue, Suite 801, Toronto, Ontario M5V 2K4
or c/o Publishers Group West
1700 Fourth Street, Berkeley CA 94710

We acknowledge for their financial support of our publishing program the Canada
Council for the Arts, the Government of Canada through the Canada Book Fund
(CBF) and the Ontario Arts Council.

 Canada Council **Conseil des Arts**
for the Arts **du Canada**   **ONTARIO ARTS COUNCIL**
CONSEIL DES ARTS DE L'ONTARIO

Library and Archives Canada Cataloguing in Publication
Gay, Marie-Louise
Summer in the city / Marie-Louise Gay and David Homel.
ISBN 978-1-55498-177-9
I. Homel, David II. Title.
PS8563.A868S85 2012   jC813'.54   C2011-906223-2

Design by Michael Solomon
Printed and bound in Canada

To our friends and neighbors in Montreal

My Adventures

1. The Case of the Missing Cat 19

2. Wilderness Camping 38

3. The Disappearing Fish 55

4. Stowaways 67

5. The Storm of the Century 80

6. The Furry Triplets 97

7. The Disappearing Brother 109

8. King for a Day 128

The "stay-cation"

BLA - BLA - BLA   BLA-BLA-BLA

*H*elp! My brain is melting!

It's as hot as an oven in here, even if all the windows in my classroom are open. Outside, the birds are singing, and the insects are droning on and on. Exactly like Mrs. Billington. She's my teacher who uses chalk for make-up and always has this fierce, bug-eyed look on her face. Especially when she starts talking about "the importance of preparing for final exams…"

Like right now.

"I want all of you to review! Revise! Make a List of Your Priorities!"

She's waving her arms around like a windmill,

and her red face is streaked with chalk. She takes a deep breath, as if she's about to say something incredibly important.

"THE RESULTS OF THESE EXAMS WILL DECIDE THE REST OF YOUR LIFE!"

That's enough to melt anybody's brain.

Adults are so weird. I'm finishing sixth grade and I'm supposed to think about the rest of my life? I just want to get out of here so I can play baseball. The rest of my life can wait.

My mother's always asking me in her casual I'm-not-really-asking-you kind of way what I want to do when I get older. As if I didn't know she wants me to say, "I want to be an artist just like you!"

But if I said that, the next minute I'd be enrolled in Saturday morning art classes, like it or not.

Or if I answered, "I'd like to be a doctor," I'd end up in young scientists' camp before I could say "Open heart surgery."

No, the rest of my life can wait until after summer vacation.

That gets me thinking. I wonder where we'll be going this summer?

You see, whether I want to or not, year after year, vacation after vacation, my parents bundle us into a car or a plane, and off we go to some out-of-the-way place.

Ever been caught in a revolution in Mexico with

kids not much older than you pointing rusty old guns in your direction? I have.

Ever been chased by raging bulls around a square in some tiny village in the south of France? Tell me about it!

If we're not riding out hurricanes on the coast, we're getting sandblasted in the desert. Or coming face to face with hungry alligators in the middle of a swamp in the middle of nowhere.

Those are the kinds of vacations we have. No lazing around on the beach. No Disneyland. Our specialty is roughing it in some faraway place. If I had the choice, which I never do, I'd have a normal kind of vacation in a normal vacation spot.

But that would never happen in my family. Not with my parents.

This year, something fishy is going on. Usually, by the end of school, our living room is buried under a mountain of maps and guidebooks (*Off the Beaten Track — Way Off,* or *Places to Go Where Nobody Goes,* or *101 Dangerous Things to Do on Your Vacation*), open suitcases, backpacks, hiking boots, diarrhea cures, mosquito repellant, rain ponchos — you name it.

But this year? Nothing. The living room is empty and my parents haven't made their usual great announcement.

I wonder what's up?

Tonight, just as we sat down to supper, my father suddenly put on his serious face.

You know that look. It happens when your parents want to tell you something important, but don't quite know how to go about it. The serious look is supposed to make you pay attention. And it works.

I have to admit, I was a little worried. Was someone sick? Were my parents getting a divorce?

As usual, my little brother Max didn't notice anything. He was trying to slip an olive to our cat, who was parked under the kitchen table. Miro will eat anything: Brussels sprouts, avocados, pickles —

anything! My mother calls him the feline vacuum cleaner.

Then my father cleared his throat in his serious way.

"Boys," he said.

Max straightened on his chair and put on an innocent look. We are definitely not allowed to feed the cat at the table.

"Boys, we've been thinking about the summer."

I waited for the big announcement about where we were heading this time. You could hear a pin drop. Or was that Miro chewing on his olive?

My father looked at my mother. He always does that when he can't quite say something difficult, like the time our last cat died, the one we had before Miro.

My mother took over.

"We've decided we're going to spend the summer in the city this year," she said. "There are plenty of things to do in Montreal. We'll be tourists, but in our own city."

"It's called a stay-cation," my father chimed in. "You're on vacation, but you stay home. Get it?"

I got it, all right. We weren't going anywhere after all.

"How come?" my brother asked. "What's going on?"

"We just thought we'd change things this year,"

my mother said. But I could tell there was something she wasn't saying.

"Actually, we haven't had very much work lately," my father explained. "So when we got some job offers for the summer, we thought we'd better accept."

"Which means we have to stay home," my mother finished.

I looked at Max, and he looked at me. I didn't know what he was thinking, but I knew what I thought.

Every year we went on some crazy trip to some off-the-beaten-track place. I always complained, but I always ended up having great adventures.

That wasn't going to happen this summer. I felt sort of empty, like when you wait all week for the championship ballgame, and then it rains.

"What do you think, boys?"

I shrugged. I didn't know what to say. And anyway, did I have a choice?

"Can we eat now?" Max asked.

Typical. My brother's brain is in his stomach.

When dinner was over, I went onto the front porch. I looked at the empty street and the red brick houses across the way. Was this supposed to be a change? No way. I lived here every day of the year. I knew every detail by heart. I knew Mr. Plouffe, the neighbor across the street, would come out the next minute to water his lawn. And he did.

This wasn't going to be a vacation at all. A vacation is when you go somewhere special and see new things and do stuff you've never done before. A vacation means going, not staying.

Max came outside.

"A stay-cation," I said. "I wonder where Dad got that one."

"I'd rather go on a go-cation."

Then he laughed his head off.

"Come on, Charlie. Let's go see who's in the alley." And he ran off toward the backyard with Miro hot on his heels.

I sat down on the steps and stared into space. I could hear my father singing as he did the dishes — one of those old songs from when he was a kid. "Hot town, summer in the city…" His voice could take paint off a wall, but at least he sounded happy.

Was I the only one who felt empty? As empty as the neighborhood would be when everyone else went away on vacation? There wouldn't be anyone around but Max and me.

"Charlie!" Max yelled from the backyard. "Do you want to play catch?"

I sighed. A whole summer with just my little brother. About as much fun as running a race with a stone in your shoe.

But there was one good part. This summer would be the first time *I* could decide what *I* wanted to do. I could find a summer job. Or go camping in the wilderness and see wild animals, or get shipwrecked, or solve a mystery. Or meet people from faraway countries. Maybe even save someone's life…

There was only one problem. I didn't see how I could do all those things in my boring old neighborhood.

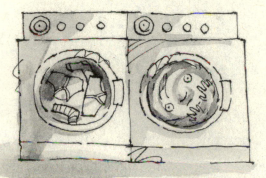

I had my first idea at the laundromat. I know, it's a weird place to hang out. But our five-hundred-year-old washing machine had just broken down again, so Mom "suggested" that I spend some of my precious vacation time making sure no one stole our clothes. As if some desperate person would stick his hands into a wildly turning machine and run off with Max's Montreal Canadiens pajamas.

So I sat there watching our underwear go around and around.

The only other person there was a little old man who seemed completely hypnotized by his clothes flopping around in the dryer. Since he was wear-

ing an undershirt and pajama bottoms, I figured that all his clothes were in the dryer. No wonder he looked worried.

To keep from dying of boredom, I started reading the signs and ads taped to the wall and the bulletin board.

For sale: One piano, one trombone, one violin, two flutes. Good condition. Cause of sale: death.

I wondered if a whole orchestra had died, or just one really talented musician.

For sale. Rocks! Dirt-cheap.

Who would pay money for a rock?

I lost my hat on Waverly Street. Great sentimental value.

On it was a picture of something that looked like a squashed burrito.

Just then, someone knocked so hard on the laundromat window that I thought it would break.

There was Max, his face squished against the glass. He stuck out his tongue, crossed his eyes and pulled on his ears. His usual clown face, only this time he left a slimy mark on the window.

"What are you doing here?" I asked.

Max wiped his mouth on his T-shirt.

"I was helping Mom with her drawings. But she told me I should come here and help you instead."

"Help me do what? Watch underwear spinning in orbit?"

"Orbit?" said Max. "Like in outer space?"

"Let me guess, Max. Was Mom having trouble with her drawing?"

"She was trying to draw a horse. I don't think she's very good at horses. So I told her to make their legs longer. That's when she told me to go help you."

Poor Max. He's so clueless sometimes.

"Look at this." I pointed to the notes on the wall. "Since we're going to be stuck in the city all summer, we might as well find a job."

"I'm too little to work."

"You can be my assistant. Here, read this."

I handed him one of the ads.

"Marcel a disparu," Max read. "Marcel has disappeared. I wonder what happened to him?"

"Maybe a magician used him in a vanishing act and can't get him to reappear. Look, they're offering a reward."

"Wow!"

I read the next one. *"Chat perdu! Lost cat! My best friend Whitey."*

Imagine if your best friend was a cat. I mean, I love Miro and everything, but I couldn't say he's my best friend.

Of course I would never tell him that. I wouldn't want to hurt his feelings.

"Hey, listen to this," I went on. *"Completely white and adorable! Call for cash reward."*

All of a sudden, Max pointed out the window.

"Look! There he is!"

Sure enough, a skinny, completely white cat was staring at us through the laundromat window. Max rushed out and grabbed him. The cat looked totally confused.

"We'd better compare him to the photo," I said.

I held up the cat next to the picture on the poster.

"It's him," Max insisted. "I'm sure it's him. We're rich!"

Just then, a girl rushed in from the sidewalk. She had messy black hair and thick black eyebrows like two caterpillars above her eyes. I'd never seen her before.

"What are you doing with my cat?" she demanded.

She grabbed Whitey from my arms and hugged him so hard he meowed. Her caterpillar eyebrows were pretty angry.

"You are cat stealers! Horrible cat stealers, both of you!"

Max was speechless. And that doesn't happen very often.

"First of all," I told her, "I think you mean cat burglars. Which we are not, by the way."

"Cat burgers?" the girl asked. "You eat cats in this country? You are truly monsters!"

Then I understood she was definitely not from here.

"We thought your cat was lost." I pointed to the sign.

"That does not look like my cat, not at all! Look at his tail. He has a black spot."

Sure enough, there was a tiny black spot at the

very end of her cat's very white tail. Though you needed a microscope to see it.

Finally, Max found his voice. "So your cat's not called Whitey?"

"Of course not. Her name is Blanquita."

And she marched out of the laundromat, holding her cat under her arm.

"What does Blanquita mean?" asked Max.

"Whitey," I told him. "But in Spanish."

I went back to reading the Lost Cat ads.

WHERE IS FROSTY?
We lost Frosty, our lovely cat.
Black with a white front. Black-and-white striped
tail. Very affectionate. Sometimes answers to Frosty.
Other times to Toasty.
Occasionally sneezes.
$50 Reward. Call 555-1CAT.

"Look at that," I said. "There's a fifty-dollar reward."

"Wow! That's a lot of money."

"Just think. If we could find two or three lost cats, and maybe a dog or two, we'd be rich. And the people who lost their pets would be happy."

As we walked home with our clean laundry, I saw more signs taped to lampposts. I had never really paid attention to them before. Nearly every post had a sign or an ad attached to it, and most of them had to do with lost animals. Some of them sounded pretty sad. If I lost Miro, I'd probably feel the same way.

"Look at all these lost pets," I told Max. "Since we don't have anything else to do, we can go looking for them. We'll look in people's backyards and under their porches. And when we find a cat that looks like one on the poster, we'll take him back to his owner and collect the reward."

"That sounds easy."

Right away he started telling me all about the things he was going to buy with his share of the reward money: comic books, a new soccer ball, ice cream bars…

"Don't spend your money till you've made it," I told him.

"And I could really use a new Super Soaker," he said. "The extra-giant model."

We spent the rest of the day walking up and down the alley.

"Frosty! Frosty!" Max called.

When that didn't work, he tried Maximilian, Queen of Sheba, Whitey, Sugarpuff and Caramel. People give their cats the funniest names.

But neither Frosty (or Toasty), Maximilian nor the Queen of Sheba came running.

After a while Max gave up. I couldn't blame him. Calling out "Sugarpuff!" in the alley sounds pretty silly.

Especially since Jean-Marie, who lives a few houses down, started making fun of Max.

"Who are you looking for? Frosty the Snowman? In the middle of summer? Ha-ha!"

"I think your mom's calling you. Jean-Mariiiiiie!" Max squealed. *"Mon petit Jean-Mariiiiiiie!"*

"Wanna eat some dandelions — raw?" Jean-Marie growled, and he grabbed a bunch of them and chased Max down the alley.

I have to admit, Max does an excellent imitation of Jean-Marie's mother.

Jean-Marie is always trying to bully Max. Every once in a while, in winter, he'll catch my little brother and wash his face with snow. But that only happens if I'm not around.

The problem with Jean-Marie is that he doesn't have any friends. Mostly because he thinks he's so great, but also because his mother makes him wear clean clothes every day, and he's not allowed to get dirty. Not to mention the way she makes him comb his hair, with a perfect line right down the middle.

"Jean-Mariiiiiiiie!" his mother yelled from their back porch. "Come and wash your hands!"

Jean-Marie sighed and trudged back to his house. Poor guy. You had to feel sorry for him.

Every time we called for cats outside our neighbor Madame Valentino's house, she gave us a suspicious look through the window. She's a math teacher, and she has a cat named Romeo. She doesn't let him outside, but every once in a while he manages to escape, and the first thing he does is run over to our house to pick a fight with Miro.

You know that expression, "The fur is flying?" That's Miro and Romeo. Then Madame Valentino rushes over and yells at us for letting Miro attack her precious, delicate Romeo.

On the third day of our job, we still hadn't found a single lost cat or dog. Max had nearly lost his voice shouting "Frosty!" up and down the alleys.

"Maybe we should get another job," he croaked.

I didn't see what else we could do. When I told our parents about our summer job, of course Dad started telling us all about the summer jobs he had when he was a kid, back in the Stone Age. Paperboy, grass-cutter, weed-puller. He even went up and down the street with a wagon, knocking on people's doors and asking them for their empty pop bottles. Every bottle was worth two cents back then, he told us, and if you collected three you could buy a candy bar, and still get some change back.

If there's one thing my father loves to do, it's tell stories from when he was our age.

But none of his old jobs would work on our street. A grownup delivers the paper from the open window of his car. And all the lawns are tiny, or covered with flowers and rock gardens. And pop comes in cans, and everyone takes their bottles back to the store for the deposit.

It looked as though we were stuck chasing after lost dogs and cats.

Then, all of a sudden, our luck changed.

"Look! It's Frosty!" Max shouted.

We were skateboarding down the sidewalk when we saw a cat sitting on a neighbor's front lawn. We both hopped off.

"I'm sure that's him."

Before I knew it, Max started crawling across the grass on all fours.

"Here, Frosty. Here, Toasty."

The cat didn't look very lost to me, but he did walk over to Max and sniff his hand. Then he purred like a tiny lawnmower. Then he let Max pick him up.

I dug into my back pocket and took out the descriptions of the lost animals. I always carried them with me, just in case.

A black cat with a white front. A black-and-white striped tail. He was affectionate and he answered to the name of Frosty—sometimes, anyway. He wasn't sneezing, but we had four out of five clues.

"It's Frosty. I know it is," Max said. "We're rich! How much is the reward?"

I looked at the paper. "Fifty dollars."

"Wow! Let's go call."

Luckily, Miro was outside, so we put Frosty in the kitchen and gave him a bowl of milk. While Max petted him and thought about all the things he was going to buy with his share of the money, I dialed the number.

"Hello?"

A woman answered. She sounded as if she were in a big hurry.

"Did you lose your cat Frosty?"

"Why, yes."

"We found him," I told her.

"Really? That's incredible!" Her voice changed entirely. "Bring him over right away, please. I'll be so happy to have my Frosty back."

She gave me an address on Rockland Avenue, one street over.

"Come on, Frosty," Max said to the cat. "Time to go home. You're not lost anymore."

We headed over to Rockland with Frosty in Max's arms. On the way, we saw the girl from the laundromat sitting on the front steps of her house. Blanquita was sitting next to her. When the girl saw us, she grabbed her cat and glared at us.

"Are you stealing cats again?"

I sighed. We were getting a bad reputation.

"It's my summer job," I told her.

"You get paid for stealing cats?"

"No, no. We find cats. Then we get paid."

"Oh. I wondered why you were yelling funny words all day, like Sugarpuff and Caramel. I thought it was some weird game you play in this city."

Then she smiled.

Max tugged at my T-shirt. Frosty was squirming and twisting in his arms like a snake.

"We have to go," I told her. "I'll see you around." I took a couple of steps, then stopped. "Hey, what's your name anyway?"

"Flor," she said, and smiled again.

"See you around, Flor!"

As we turned onto the next street, Max asked, "Her name's Floor?"

"Not Floor. Flor! It means flower in Spanish."

"Oh-la-la," said Max, which doesn't make any sense, since "oh-la-la" is French.

Meanwhile, Frosty was doing his best to wriggle out of Max's arms.

"Do something," he said in a panic. "If he gets away, we'll never catch him again."

I took Frosty from Max. For a cat that was supposed to be affectionate, he had pretty sharp claws. By some miracle I managed to hold onto him all the way to Rockland Avenue. I only ended up with a few scratches on my arms.

Max rang the doorbell, and a tall, skinny woman stepped out. She looked very, very excited.

Until she saw the cat.

"That's not Frosty," she said. "Oh, and here I was so happy…"

I thought she was going to cry right then and there.

"Sure it's Frosty," Max told her. "Look! A black cat with a white front, and a black-and-white striped tail. He even came when we called his name."

"But it's not the same black, and it's not the same white. And this one's tail is different."

"You could take him anyway," Max suggested.

"Are you *sure* it's not your cat?" I asked.

"Believe me, I know my Frosty."

Then she closed the door. We walked down the street very slowly, with the cat that wasn't Frosty following close behind.

I bent down, picked up the cat and looked him in the eye.

"Okay, if you're not Frosty, who are you? Are you lost or not? Tell me the truth."

"Snowball!" a man called from across the street. "Come here right now!"

The cat jumped out of my arms and ran straight to the man. He picked him up.

"I told you not to talk to strangers," he scolded his cat.

A black cat named Snowball?

Max and I looked at each other and shrugged. Another day's work, and no reward. At this rate, summer would be over before we made any money.

As we turned onto our street, I saw a small crowd of people standing underneath our maple tree, staring up.

"Oh, my poor Romeo!" someone was yelling. "*Viens ici, mon Roméo.* Come to my arms, Romeo!"

It wasn't Juliet. It was Madame Valentino from next door. Her precious Romeo had escaped again and climbed up our maple tree. Maybe Miro chased him.

Whatever had happened, he was stuck now. Old Mr. Plouffe from across the street was trying to tempt him down with a piece of dry bread.

What did Mr. Plouffe think? That the cat was a pigeon? Flor was there with Blanquita in her arms.

I knew how I could rescue Romeo! I shinnied up the trunk and climbed from branch to branch until I reached the one he was clinging to.

Then I realized I had a problem. How was I going to hold Romeo and climb down the tree at the same time?

I called to Max, "I need a bag."

Max can actually be quick when he wants to. He dashed into the house.

Meanwhile, Jean-Marie showed up.

"Are you stuck? Should I call the fire department?" he sneered.

"You're just mad because you're not allowed to climb trees," I said, just as his mother stuck her head out their front door.

"Jean-Mariiiiiie!!! Time for your piano lesson!" she screeched.

Jean-Marie kicked the tree trunk and walked away.

At the foot of the tree, Madame Valentino was still crying, "Oh, my poor Romeo! *Ô, mon pauvre chéri!*" It was really irritating.

Then Max's head popped out the second-floor window. My mother was standing behind him.

"Be careful, Charlie," she called.

Obviously, I thought.

"Here you go," Max shouted.

He threw me my school backpack, without any books in it, luckily. I caught it with my free hand. Then I reached out, grabbed Romeo by his tiny pink polka-dot collar and stuffed him into my open backpack before he could say "Meow." I slung the bag over my shoulder and climbed down as fast as I could.

At the foot of the tree, Madame Valentino was practically in tears.

"Thank you. Oh, thank you, young man. I'm so happy to see there are still a few nice children left."

"De rien, Madame," I said in my most polite French.

Then she took Romeo out of my bag and went into her house.

"Nice job, Charlie," Mr. Plouffe said. As he wandered back to his house, he nibbled on his piece of bread.

"Charlie!" said Max, very excited. "We saved a cat's life!"

Well, technically speaking, *I* had saved the cat's life. True, Max did help a little.

I began to think. Maybe I could turn my experience into a summer job. I could just see the ad taped to the wall of the laundromat.

CAT EMERGENCY!
Does your cat need to be rescued?
Is your cat in mortal danger?
Call Charlie the Cat Saver!
Fee: negotiable
(514) 555-CATS

Just then I heard Madame Valentino's front door open. She called me over.

"Here, young man. This is for saving my Romeo."

She handed me an apple. It was pretty wrinkled. One of her students probably gave it to her to get on her good side.

Now it was my salary for my first summer job. And I had to share it with my brother!

TWO
Miro vs. the wild animals

I decided to take a day off work. No searching for
lost cats, dogs or anything else.

I figured I'd finish reading *Robinson Crusoe*.
Have you ever read it? It's all about a man who gets
shipwrecked on a desert island. He builds a hut and
a raft, raises goats and dries grapes to make raisins.
He fights off cannibals and even meets a friend he
calls Friday.

If I lived on a desert island, I would —

"Charlie!" my mother called. "Come down,
we're having a council of war."

That's her way of saying the family is getting together to discuss something. What it really means

is that I never get to have a moment to myself.

I went down to the kitchen. Everyone was sitting around the table: my mom, my father, Max, even Miro.

I should have known! No sooner had my parents decided we weren't going anywhere for summer vacation than they started telling me what to do.

First, my mother suggested day camp.

"Are you kidding?" I asked her. "I just finished school. Teachers have been bossing me around all year. Do you think I want to be bossed around by camp counselors singing songs about ninety-nine bottles of beer on the wall? And those shirts! We all have to wear the same T-shirts so we won't get lost."

Then my father came up with the idea of swimming lessons.

"You're the one who needs swimming lessons," I said. "Not me."

My father can barely dog-paddle, and only in the shallow end of the pool. He told me once that when he was a kid he had a really mean swimming teacher who believed in the "sink or swim" method. He threw all his students into the pool *before* they'd learned to swim. No wonder my father doesn't like the water! The kids should have ganged up on the teacher and thrown *him* into the water, whistle and all.

"Well," my father answered, "you can always learn to swim better. The YMCA has a pool, and…"

"Listen," I said. "This is my vacation and I'll decide what I want to do."

"All right," my mother asked. "What *do* you want to do?"

"Actually, I wouldn't mind going camping in the wilderness. And while I'm at it, maybe learn some survival skills and meet a few wild animals. Meanwhile, you can send Max to day camp, and he can learn how to dive instead of belly-flopping."

Then my father came up with one of his great ideas.

"Why don't you go camping in the backyard? I used to do that when I was a kid. It was a blast."

A blast. Kids probably said that in the 1960s. Or the 1860s, more like it.

But maybe it wasn't such a bad idea. At least I'd be on my own like Robinson Crusoe. Maybe I could even build a fire and —

"We're going camping! We're going camping!"

Max started jumping up and down. My parents had big smiles on their faces.

My heart sank. There was no way I could get out of this. Max would be coming with me whether I liked it or not.

"Okay, okay," I said. "Come on, Friday. Let's go find the tent."

Max and I went down to the basement. That's where we keep everything that a) we don't need anymore, b) is broken and we can't fix and c) we never needed in the first place. There was the brand-new exercise bicycle that my mother bought for my father because she wanted him to lose weight. There were our school projects and art masterpieces, like the plasticine solar system I made in second grade, which looked like a bunch of dried worms now. Or the noodle-and-bottle-cap art project Max made in daycare. At the time, my parents thought they were works of genius. There were boxes of old books that my father kept meaning to give to the library. Fondue sets, broken lamps, a tiny black-and-white TV with rabbit ears, which is how people watched television before satellites were invented.

And somewhere was a tent. There had to be. After all, everything else was down here.

We started digging through the piles of junk.

Half an hour later, Max popped out from behind Miro's caved-in scratching couch. He had spider webs in his hair.

"I found it!" He pulled a khaki-colored bundle into the middle of the basement. A cloud of dust rose into the air.

"I think we'd better open it outside."

He took one end and I took the other, and we

climbed the stairs and went through the kitchen to the back door. When Max accidentally stepped on Miro, my mother came down from her studio.

"Charlie! Where are you going with that?"

"Outside."

"Good. Make sure it stays there."

She looked unhappily at the floor. The tent was shedding dried mud the way Miro sheds fur in the summer.

We started unfolding the bundle of canvas in the backyard. Not only was the tent covered in dried mud, but mold was growing on parts of it.

"Wow, it sure stinks!" Max complained.

"Somebody must have put it away while it was still wet."

We spread it out and discovered a jumble of pegs and ropes and metal pieces.

I'm not exactly a camping specialist. I've never even gone camping. But putting up a tent just takes a little calm thinking.

That's when my father appeared.

"I was a boy scout when I was young. You could win a badge for putting up a tent in the fastest time."

He looked at the tent and scratched his chin.

"Okay! Let's get to work," he said, and he clapped his hands.

An hour later, I realized that Dad had never

earned the "Tent" badge. The tent still looked like
a pile of dirty laundry.

Luckily for us, the phone rang.

"I'm sure you guys will be able to figure it out.
Sorry, I have to go!"

Then he ran inside, looking very relieved.

I found some metal rods under the tent floor.
They turned out to be the frame. I pulled the ropes
tight, then nailed the pegs into the ground. Com-
pared to my father, I was a tent genius.

After another half hour's worth of arguments
with Max, I finally got the thing standing. True,

it was a little crooked, and it did look like a strong wind might blow it over. But with a little luck, there wouldn't be any strong winds.

We left the flaps open to air out the tent.

"Now what?" my brother asked.

"Now we wait for darkness."

We packed our bags before supper, and afterward we moved into the tent with all the necessary equipment. Sleeping bags and pillows, flashlights, mosquito repellant, enough books to start our own library, four granola bars, some boxes of raisins, peanut butter and banana sandwiches and a bag of chocolate cookies. My brother brought his stuffed penguin, of course, and his rubber insect collection inside a pillowcase.

"We'll have real bugs. You don't need those," I told him.

Max wanted to bring the bread knife in case bears or wolves attacked, but my father wouldn't let him.

"You might cut yourself."

"Or me," I added.

"I can come and visit you later if you like," my father said.

"Just to say goodnight," my mother added.

"That's okay," Max told her. "We'll be all right on our own."

Since we were going camping, I figured I should

bring some ghost stories and tales of horror. You know, the kind of books that begin with "It was a dark and stormy night…" I grabbed *Dracula* off my shelf. On the way out, I took *Bunnicula*, too. That way, if the real *Dracula* was too scary for Max, I could read him *Bunnicula*, since it's about a vampire rabbit. How scary could that be?

Once it got really dark, I read some of the scary parts of *Dracula* to Max. But soon he started clicking his flashlight on and off and shining it in my face. Next he put it under his chin and made horrible faces and groaning noises. Our two-man pup tent started to feel a little small.

"Let's play flashlight tag," I said.

Flashlight tag is like any other tag, except that you tag the other person with the beam of your light. I was It, of course, and Max ran off to hide in the dark. I charged up and down the alley and in and out of the neighbors' yards looking for him. Max is so small he can hide behind a garbage can or a narrow tree trunk.

Finally I spotted him behind the recycling box and tagged him with my light.

"Got you! You're It!" I cried.

"No way, you missed."

He ran off into the darkness. Sometimes he's really a bad sport.

Madame Valentino stormed onto her back

porch next door. If there's one thing she hates, it's kids. That's probably why she became a teacher.

"You boys! Get off my property! You should be in bed! Where are your parents?"

We threw ourselves flat on the ground behind her lilac bush.

"Follow me," I whispered to Max, "we'll crawl back under the fence. If she catches us, she'll probably give us homework."

Max giggled loudly.

"*Qui est là?*" she called. "Who's there? I'm going to call the police."

Okay, we didn't have any bears or wolves on our camping trip, but we did have Madame Valentino. She's pretty ferocious!

I crawled under the fence into our yard. I waited and waited, but Max didn't show up. What was he doing? When he finally slithered back under the fence, he was holding a big bunch of daisies. They looked as though they'd just crawled under the fence, too.

"A present for Mom!" Max beamed.

"I'm not so sure she'd want a bunch of muddy daisies you stole from the neighbor's garden," I told him.

I guess he saw my point, because he slipped down the alley and threw the flowers into Jean-Marie's backyard.

"There! Madame Valentino will think he did it," Max whispered.

We climbed inside our tent and decided to read a little. Unfortunately, we'd used up our batteries playing flashlight tag.

"I don't need light to have a snack," Max pointed out. "I can find my mouth in the dark."

Three packages of raisins, one sandwich and a couple cookies later, he fell asleep.

I lay on top of my sleeping bag because it was too warm to be inside it. In the darkness, I listened to the wind in the tree branches. They were rattling back and forth and creaking high above my head.

It was a good thing Max was asleep. He'd probably say there was a monster outside, and make me go out and check.

Suddenly, I heard something rustling in the bushes right beside our tent. Then the rustling stopped, and a scratching noise began. And then… the sound of someone eating.

Who was having a late-night snack in our back-yard?

The rustling, snuffling sound was very close. It sounded like someone — or something — was pulling out clumps of grass around the tent.

Maybe that something was trying to get into our tent.

Remember, I told myself, *there are no man-eating animals in Montreal.*

Just then Max woke up. He sat up right next to me. He was breathing really hard.

"Charlie!" he whispered. "What is it? A bear?"

"I don't know," I whispered back. "Don't move. I'll have a look."

Very sl-o-w-ly, I unzipped the tent flap. I peered out. The air was still warm, and the moon had come out, lighting up our backyard. Two beady black eyes looked back at me. The moonlight shone on a large white stripe that ran from a small head to the tip of a tail.

A skunk! Right outside our tent!

I tried to close the flap, but the zipper was stuck.

"What is it, Charlie?" Max asked.

"Sssh! It's only a skunk."

"Let me see," Max insisted.

He tried to crawl past me. He probably wanted to do his grizzly bear imitation to scare it away.

That would mean only one thing: disaster. The skunk would get scared, and everyone knows what scared skunks do. They give you a skunk-shower.

I grabbed Max by the legs and jumped on him to keep him from getting outside. Through the open tent flap, the skunk gave us this look — half-curious and half-unhappy — as if it didn't know what to think about these strange creatures in the

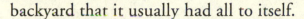

backyard that it usually had all to itself.

Suddenly, I heard a long howl and a hiss, and another wild animal appeared. A large furry creature with gray and white stripes.

Miro! He was perched on the birdbath, his tail slicing the air. He had come to defend his territory.

"Miro, I don't think…"

But he didn't listen. He pounced on the skunk. I held my breath, which was a really good idea, because then it happened: the worst smell in the world. The skunk sprayed Miro. He howled and ran off toward the house, and the skunk disappeared down the alley. The next minute I heard it knocking over Madame Valentino's metal garbage cans.

Poor Miro! With all the commotion, my father woke up, and he switched on the backyard light.

"Miro got skunked," I called to him.

"Yes, Charlie, I figured that out by myself. Don't worry. I know what to do."

The next minute my father came out into the yard with a big bucket and a giant container of white vinegar. He poured the vinegar into the bucket and mixed it with water. Then he picked up the smelliest cat in Montreal and started washing him.

Maybe Dad never got the Tent-Raising badge in boy scouts, but I bet he earned the Cat-Washing one.

"What about tomato juice?" I asked. "I thought that's how you de-skunk a cat."

"That's only in stories. You need something really acidic to get rid of the smell. And there's more acid in vinegar."

Miro didn't even complain. Maybe he knew that a vinegar bath is good for cats that have gotten too close to skunks.

When the bath was over, Miro hopped out of the bucket and jumped onto the picnic table. He started shaking himself like mad, trying to get rid of every last drop of vinegar.

After a short pillow fight, Max fell asleep again. The wind was starting to blow harder, and it was easy to imagine I was Robinson Crusoe. *I saw the sea come after me as high as a great hill, and as furious as an enemy*, he wrote. It was a good thing he knew how to swim, since he was able to make it onto the shore of his desert island. I wondered if I would have the strength to fight the waves if I were shipwrecked.

Suddenly the sky lit up with lightning, and there was a roll of thunder. The wind tossed the trees, and small branches and twigs rained down on the tent.

A summer storm!

I pictured the dangers. A tree could fall on the tent. I could get struck by lightning. The skunk could come back looking for shelter in our tent.

But I'd forgotten the biggest danger of all. Max.

He woke up and reached for his flashlight.

"It doesn't work," he complained.

"With all this lightning, who needs a flashlight?"

"I'm going in. Besides, it stinks out here. I've had enough!"

"It's all part of the fun. The rain will wash away the skunk smell."

Max didn't see it that way. He gathered up what was left of his snacks and climbed out of the tent.

Just then, the skies opened. Buckets of rain poured down on Max, who was locked out of the house, since our father had forgotten to leave the back door open. By the time he came downstairs and opened the door, my brother looked just like Miro after his vinegar bath.

Exactly one minute later, the rain stopped and the moon came out again. I opened the flap to air out the tent. I wasn't sleepy at all anymore.

I went and sat on the picnic table and listened to the sounds of the night. It really was a very busy place. Crickets and peepers were sending insect messages to each other. The night bus went by on Van Horne Avenue, its brakes squealing. In the train yard at the end of the street, freight cars were banging together. I wondered where that train was going.

I sat so quietly that a raccoon jumped up onto the picnic table right next to me. When it saw me, it gave me a surprised look from behind its little thief's mask, but it didn't drop the piece of watermelon in its mouth. It had probably picked it out of Madame Valentino's garbage.

"Aren't you going to wash it first?" I asked. "I thought you guys always washed your food."

The raccoon cocked its head and looked at me, as if it were trying to understand.

"Of course you don't have to wash it. It's watermelon."

But the raccoon didn't get my joke. It finished chewing on the watermelon and left the rind on the table next to me, then jumped down and disappeared into the bushes.

From the end of the alley, I heard shouting and

laughing and the sound of wheels on pavement. A minute later, a long line of skateboarders rode past my yard, with flashing lights attached to their helmets and their backpacks.

I pulled on my jeans and walked over to Van Horne and watched them disappear, gliding down the hill, their lights fading into the darkness. I wished I were with them. Riding through the city on a warm night, on a skateboard, with your friends. Now that would be an adventure!

But, wait. I could try it myself. I got my spare flashlight from the tent — the one I didn't tell Max about — and my skateboard from the back porch. I started down the alley with the moon riding above me among the tree branches. I looked into the houses as I went past. Almost every one of them had the television on. Cats raced across the alleyway — probably the lost cats we were looking for. I heard heavy metal music blaring out of an apartment window.

I felt like I was spying on the world like an invisible bat, swooping from one alley to the next.

Finally, I headed home, to my tent in the wilderness of my backyard. My house was dark, and everyone was asleep. Everyone but me.

THREE
The fun of fish-sitting

All of a sudden, my luck changed. Catherine, the girl from a couple houses down, was going to Maine with her parents for two weeks. When I went to Maine, we got caught in a huge hurricane. I wondered if the same thing might happen to her. Maybe she'd be gone for longer than two weeks.

She asked Max and me to take care of her fish. Now that sounded like an easy job!

Think of all the things you don't have to do when you babysit a goldfish.

You don't have to make it stop watching TV. You don't have to help it with its homework. You don't have to read it a bedtime story or kiss it good-night (yuck!).

All Max and I had to do was feed the fish once a day, and change its water and clean its bowl once in a while. How hard could that be? We would still have plenty of time to look for lost cats and dogs. The fish would be our part-time job.

The first thing we did was move Jaws, her goldfish, over to our house. Catherine gave Max and me a list of instructions a mile long about how to take care of Jaws. We had to talk to him and play his favorite CDs, because he just loved music.

"Fish don't answer to their names," she told us. "But my father's allergic to fur, so that's the only kind of pet I can have."

"Don't worry, Catherine. Your fish will be fine."

"Don't feed him too much. Fish don't know when to stop eating."

"I'll remember that."

The very next afternoon, I caught Max feeding Jaws for the third time that day.

"Stop feeding him, fish-brain. Remember what Catherine said."

"But he hasn't eaten since lunch. And look, he's smacking his lips."

"He's going to get fat," I warned Max.

"I eat all the time and I never get fat."

"Yeah. But you're not a fish."

Of course Max immediately started doing his fish imitation. He put his hands next to his ears as if they were gills. Then he made popping noises with his mouth and bugged out his eyes. Not very convincing, if you ask me.

Jaws didn't look very convinced, either.

It turns out the more you feed a goldfish, the more it needs to go to the bathroom. And the sooner you have to change its water.

After a few days, the water in the fish bowl started to turn cloudy. It didn't look very appetizing. I mean, who would want to swim around in… you-know-what.

"You'd better change the water," I told Max, "since you're the one who's always feeding him."

That's one thing I learned about summer jobs. Always get your assistant to do the dirty work.

To my amazement, Max agreed right away.

He grabbed the fish bowl and marched into the bathroom. The water sloshed back and forth, and Jaws looked a little seasick. When I spotted Miro running into the bathroom after them, I knew something bad was going to happen.

I caught up to Max standing over the toilet, talking to Miro. Max was hanging onto the bowl with one hand while he held back the fish with the other.

"So, Miro, first you have to get rid of the dirty water. And fast, because then you have to put in clean water right away. Otherwise, the fish — uh-oh!"

Splash! Jaws was in the toilet. I wasn't even surprised.

"Charlie!" my brother wailed.

"Whatever you do, don't flush."

"Thanks a lot!" Max looked as though he were about to burst into tears.

"There's a fishing pole in the basement somewhere. I think it's behind the tent."

"You're no help at all!" Max's lower lip started to tremble.

All three of us — Max, Miro and I — watched Jaws swimming around in the toilet. He didn't look very happy, and I couldn't blame him.

"Fill the bowl up with clean water," I told Max. "I'll grab Jaws and put him back in."

"You're going to put your hand in the toilet?"

"Can you think of another way?"

Max didn't answer. He filled up Jaws' bowl while I went fishing — with my hand. I grabbed for Jaws once or twice, but the goldfish was pretty fast. He slipped away every time.

"Do something, Charlie!"

"Come on, Jaws. It's for your own good."

Finally, on my sixth try, I grabbed hold of the

fish. I think Jaws was getting tired. I sure was. I lifted him out of the toilet and was about to drop him back into his bowl when he flipped his tail and jumped right out of my hand.

Have you ever heard that expression *a slippery fish*? That's exactly what Jaws was.

The fish hit the bathroom floor with a *plop!* and started twitching around on the tiles. Miro took a swipe at him. Luckily, he missed.

It was even harder to pick the fish off the floor

than out of the water. Miro pounced again and pinned Jaws down. I grabbed the fish from Miro's claws and dumped him back into his bowl. Miro looked disappointed.

"You saved his life!" Max shouted.

I looked at Jaws. He didn't seem grateful, but I couldn't be sure. He didn't have a lot of expression on his face.

Then I washed my hands. Three times in a row.

The next morning, I took a vacation from looking after Max and Jaws, and I stayed in my room and read. I had finished *Robinson Crusoe* and started *The Wizard of Earthsea*. It's about a kid who finds out he has an incredible magic power that he can hardly control, and…

"Charlie! Come and see Jaws' new trick!"

Max is about as irritating as an alarm clock when you're trying to go back to sleep. But this morning I decided to hit the Snooze button. Or was that the Ignore button? Anyway, I didn't answer.

"Hey, Charlie, I know you heard me. So don't pretend!" Max yelled from downstairs.

"Charlie!" That was my mother in her studio. "Would you please, please, *please* go see what Max wants?"

I put down my book. There was no way to get any peace and quiet in this house. If I didn't rush downstairs right away to find out what was happening, my mother would explode from her studio, so I might as well get it over with.

There was Max standing in the kitchen by the fish bowl.

"Look! Jaws can swim on his back."

The fish was floating on the surface of the water.

"He's not doing the backstroke, Max. He's dead."

Max stuck his finger in the water and pushed the fish a little, as if he were trying to wake him up.

"We're in trouble! We killed Catherine's best friend."

"*You* killed him," I said. "*You* fed him too much. Then *you* dropped him in the toilet."

"What do we do now?"

"I don't know. I guess we'd better bury him."

I trudged upstairs to get dressed. I was wondering how we'd explain it all to Catherine when she got home.

Just then my mother came out of her studio. She always says she hates to be disturbed by Max and me, but whenever something happens in the house, she wants to know exactly what's going on.

"Now what is it?" she asked.

"Bad news. Jaws died."

She put her hand over her mouth, as if the goldfish had been a close member of the family.

"I'm so sorry."

"Me, too. I don't know how we'll tell Catherine. She's going to be really mad."

"She'll certainly be disappointed," my mother agreed.

"And we won't get paid, either."

My mother went back into her studio.

Was that it? Wasn't she going to come up with a solution?

I wandered out onto the front porch, feeling useless. So far, my summer jobs had been total disasters. I found the wrong cats for the wrong people. Then we killed our neighbor's goldfish. Even if Max had done it, I was still a little responsible.

I decided to go for a walk. Max appeared on the porch, and of course I had to take him. Looking after him was the hardest job of all, and I didn't even get paid for it. We went past the corner store, then the laundromat. On the next block, there was a pet shop. We stopped and looked in the window.

There were two big aquariums. One was full of colorful tropical fish darting around in all directions. Some of them were so thin you could see right through them.

The other aquarium was full of goldfish doing nothing in particular except staring out the window.

And you know what? The fish all looked the same.

"Come on, Max, let's go shopping."

He followed me into the pet shop. Kittens were meowing, puppies were barking and hamsters were running like crazy on their wheels. The smell wasn't exactly great, and I didn't like to see all the ani-

mals cooped up like that. The kittens and puppies pressed their noses against the sides of their cages, looking at me with big, begging eyes that said, "I'm adorable. Take me home!"

The pet-shop owner was pretending to be busy, sorting chewy dog treats, but he was watching us like a hawk. He glared at us from under his bristly eyebrows.

What did he think? That I'd grab a fish and stuff it into my pocket?

"Can I help you?" he asked grumpily.

"We need a goldfish," I said.

"Let's get one of those striped fishies," Max piped up.

"*Pterophyllum scalare*," said the man. "A tropical fish from the Amazon River, commonly known as an angelfish?"

It was probably the most expensive fish in the store.

"Yeah, the red and blue one," Max said.

"No. We're getting a goldfish."

"An angelfish is prettier," Max whined.

"Maybe so, but what are you going to tell Catherine? Sorry, but while you were on vacation, your goldfish morphed into an angelfish?"

He stuck out his lower lip and sulked a little. But I was right, and he knew it.

"You need to replace someone's fish?" the pet-shop man asked. "What did it look like?"

"I don't know. He was your average goldfish."

"His name was Jaws," Max added.

"Original name," the man admitted.

"He had this kind of goldfish look," I said. "You know, you never knew what he was thinking, or whether he was happy or not."

"Except when he fell in the toilet. Then he didn't look so happy," Max chimed in.

"He didn't *fall* into the toilet. You *dropped* him in because you — "

"Could you be more precise?" the pet-shop man said. "What kind of fins did it have?"

Max and I shrugged. "Goldfish fins."

The man frowned. "Were they black like this?" He pointed to one fish. "Or gold all over like that?"

I wasn't completely sure. I didn't remember Jaws having black fins, but I didn't remember him not having black fins, either. But it was important. The new fish had to look exactly like the old one.

"Try and remember, Max. You should know. You spent more time with him. After all, you fed him five times a day."

The man rolled his eyes. "Typical," he muttered.

I guess Max wasn't the only fish-killer in the neighborhood.

Finally, Max and I decided on the most ordinary-looking fish in the tank. Gold with gold fins, and a fishy look on its face. The man scooped it out of the aquarium with a net and put it in a plastic bag full of water. I paid for it with the last of my money. At least goldfish aren't that expensive.

The man handed me the bag. "Whatever you do, don't drop him, don't throw him in the toilet and don't overfeed him."

He followed us to the door and stared at us through the shop window until we crossed the street, like he was about to call the pet police on us.

We walked back to the house. I held the bag carefully, with both hands.

"Do you really think he looks like Jaws?" Max asked.

"He looks more like Jaws than Jaws did."

FOUR
My brother, the sweet-roll thief

Summer in the city can be kind of boring. Especially when there's no one to hang out with except your little brother.

So I started this game where I invented secret identities for people. One day we skateboarded past a man pushing a stroller with a big bald baby screaming his head off.

"Check out the Martian in the stroller," I whispered to Max.

Max stopped and stared. Then he whizzed off, screaming, "The aliens are attacking! The aliens are attacking!"

The man really liked that.

Then I said, "See that lady in the high heels and the black dress carrying a violin case?"

"What about her?"

"She's from the Mafia, and that's really a machine gun."

"No way," Max said. "Prove it."

"Okay," I told him. "We'll hide behind those bushes, and when she comes past, we'll jump out and yell. She'll be so scared she'll drop her case and run away. You can look inside it yourself."

We crouched down behind the bushes. But wouldn't you know it? Just then Flor came along, and of course she saw us right away.

"Hey, why are you hiding? Looking for more cats to steal?"

I didn't want to explain my crazy game. She thought I was strange enough already.

Then the lady with the violin case walked past on her very tall high heels. Now we'd never know what was in her case!

After wrecking our great plan, Flor went away laughing and left us there, crouching in the bushes.

The next morning when I came downstairs, I spotted Max in the front yard. He was playing our game by himself, hunched down behind a bush. He kept peering out and scanning the street with Dad's binoculars.

I crept up behind him and dropped

an acorn down the back of his shirt. He jumped five feet in the air, then glared at me. He put his finger to his lips and pointed down the street.

I didn't see anything, but I did hear something. *Ding, dong, ding.* Three notes from a bell that sounded very much out of tune.

"See that orange truck?" Max whispered. "The guy inside it is an ax murderer." He ducked his head. "Here he comes. Stay down!"

An ax murderer? What was Max talking about?

The next minute, an ancient orange truck moved past our house so slowly I could have beaten it in a foot race. The truck didn't have any doors, and standing at the steering wheel was a man even

more ancient than the truck. The lines on his face were deeper than the Grand Canyon. He was steering with one hand and ringing a bell with the other.

The truck was covered with drawings of knives, scissors and axes. It stopped right in front of our house.

"Look!" Max whispered loudly. "I told you."

I could have explained to Max that it was Tony the Knife Sharpener, and not Tony the Bloodthirsty Criminal. But why not have a little fun? After all, there wasn't anything else to do.

"You're right," I said. "We'd better go investigate."

With my little brother creeping along behind me, we moved toward the truck. People were lining up by the front, holding lawn clippers and scissors and carving knives. They handed their tools to Tony, who had a sharpening wheel in the back of the old van.

"Look, Max. All our neighbors are lining up for their turn in the torture chamber."

I slipped past the line of people and climbed the first step to get a better look inside. Tony, who must have been at least a hundred years old, was wearing dark glasses that covered half his face. A heavy stone wheel was spinning really fast, and Tony was pressing a carving knife as long as a sword against the wheel. Red sparks flew into the air like fireworks. It really was something!

Then, through the shower of sparks, I saw Max. His face was squished against the back window of the truck. His wacky clown face, of course.

Just then Tony saw him, too.

"*Mamma mia!* Who's that?"

Tony jumped down from the truck and pushed past everyone. For a hundred-year-old man, he moved pretty fast. The next thing I knew, he had Max by the shirt.

"Who's this bambino climbing on my truck?"

Max was totally terrified, and I couldn't blame him. In his dark goggles and with his white hair sticking up in all directions, Tony looked like a creature from outer space. He had Max's shirt in one hand, and in the other he held a carving knife as long as Max's arm.

"Help!" Max screamed.

I decided I'd better rescue him.

"Excuse me, Mr. Tony," I said, tapping him on the shoulder.

The man turned around. "You know this bambino?"

"I'm afraid that's my brother," I admitted.

"He scared me, I'm telling you. I look up, I see this strange face, I don't know what to think."

Max was trembling like a leaf. Like a whole forest full of leaves.

"He just likes to spy a little." Though spying

on someone with a long sharp knife in his hand is never a good idea.

"I don't like spies," Tony said. "I came to this country to get away from spies."

Then he let go of Max's shirt. Without another word, Max ran straight for the house.

His career as a spy was over. And I figured that was the end of his fish-brain ideas.

But the very next day, as we were walking along Van Horne, Max and I passed a delivery truck parked outside the corner store. The driver was busy unloading loaves of bread and stacking them on a two-wheeled handcart. Then he pushed his load into the store, leaving the back of his truck open.

"Hey, I bet there are doughnuts in there!"

And believe it or not, Max jumped right into the open truck.

"Max! Get out of there!"

"Come and get me," he called back.

"You'll be sorry if I do. Now get out. Remember what happened with the last truck?"

"There isn't an ax murderer in this one."

He went and hid behind a tall stack of hamburger buns. I didn't know what to do. If Max got caught in the truck, he'd be accused of stealing, and I'd get in trouble, too, since, as usual, I was supposed to be looking after him.

"Okay, you asked for it!"

I climbed into the truck. I heard him burrowing behind the loaves of bread.

I had to get him out of there before we both ended up in jail.

"Catch me if you can," Max said.

I moved deeper into the truck. The piles of bread and buns and rolls and doughnuts were packed very close together.

Then it happened. The driver hung his two-wheeled cart inside the truck and closed the door hard. *Slam!*

"I hope you're happy, Max, wherever you are," I told him. "We're prisoners now. And we don't even know where we're going to end up."

I felt pretty strange talking to a tower of hamburger buns.

The truck lurched forward and we drove away. I had to grab onto a rack of muffins to keep from falling. We stopped at traffic lights, we turned corners, we went over bridges.

But where were we going? And what would happen to us when we got there?

A few blocks further on, I heard Max's voice, very small, from behind the sweet rolls.

"I was just joking, Charlie."

"Right. Well, the joke is on us!"

We continued driving through the city. Let me tell you, time seems very, very long when you're a prisoner in a delivery van and you don't know where you're being delivered. Except maybe to jail.

Suddenly, we stopped. The driver was whistling to himself as he opened the door and grabbed the handcart. Then he climbed into the back of the truck and went right for the sweet rolls where Max was hiding.

Like a mouse running from a cat, Max dashed right past the delivery man and jumped onto the street. I made a run for it, too.

"What the heck?" the man said.

I think he was as scared as we were. He jumped out of the truck and started running after us. But he quickly gave up. He probably didn't want to leave his bread unprotected.

"If I ever catch you stealing out of my truck again," he yelled, "I'll, I'll…"

We didn't hang around to find out what he would do.

A minute later, we were catching our breath a block away, on a busy street corner. Buses and taxis roared past, and bicycles dodged in and out of traffic. A sidewalk sale was going on, and people were pushing their way around piles of shoes and clothes, and past a guy selling shishkebabs on a stick.

We weren't going to jail after all — at least not this time.

"We got away!" Max said, very proud.

"Right," I told him. "But we have another problem. We're completely lost."

We needed a compass, or at least a map. But when I thought about it, I realized we had something better: the Mountain.

The Mountain sits right in the middle of Montreal. It's really an extinct volcano, and you can see it from just about everywhere. If you know where you live in relation to the Mountain, then you're not really lost.

I looked up and down the street. In one direction, I saw the tower of the Olympic Stadium. In the other, there was the Mountain — a *very* long way away. The street seemed to climb forever to reach it. And if we ever got there, we would only be halfway home, since we lived on the other side of the Mountain.

I pointed up the street.

"Let's go," I told Max. "I hope you like walking."

At first Max did his best to keep up with me, because he knew he had gotten us into this mess in the first place. But a few blocks later, he started dragging his feet and complaining.

"I'm tired," he whined.

"Think about that the next time you decide to hitch a ride in a bread truck."

"It was just a joke."

"You said that already."

"How far is it, Charlie?"

I pointed off into the distance. "See the Mountain? We have to walk all the way there."

Max's face fell. "It's going to take us a million years."

"And once we get there, we have to go up one side, then down the other. Too bad you don't have wings."

"Too bad we can't go through the Mountain."

I thought about what Max said. Of course we

couldn't go through the Mountain, but we could go under it. In other words, the subway. That was the fastest way around the city, according to my mother.

Now I just had to find a subway station.

I looked around and discovered we were standing in front of a fortune-teller's shop. There was a crystal ball in the window.

A very large woman wearing a very large red and gold dress and an enormous blue turban was standing in the doorway.

"Do you kids need your fortunes told?" she asked. "Madame Toussaint knows all, tells all."

"I wouldn't mind knowing where the nearest subway station is."

She pointed up the street. "Two blocks on your left. And may the spirits smile upon you."

Sure enough, after pushing and pulling Max two more blocks, we came to the Mont Royal subway.

We went down the stairs and I looked at the map. We were on the orange line. If we went north and changed to the blue line at Jean Talon, it was only four stops to Outremont, where we lived.

A piece of cake!

There was only one small problem. We didn't have any money for subway tickets.

This time Max solved the problem. Before I could say anything, he slipped underneath the barrier.

"Hey, Charlie, which way do I go?"

"Wait for me! Whatever you do, don't go anywhere!"

I could just see it. Max lost in the subway, forever.

The ticket taker was watching the whole thing from inside his glass cage.

"That's my little brother," I said to him, "and…"

"*Vas-y, mon garçon!*"

And like magic, the barrier opened!

We came out of the subway right on Van Horne Avenue, very close to our house. As we walked toward our street, believe it or not, Max pulled a sweet roll from his pocket and started chewing on it. A very crushed, slightly dusty sweet roll.

"You stole that from the truck!"

"Not really. There was a hole in one of the pack-ages. Some of the rolls fell out. This one was on the floor."

Not only a thief, but a bad liar.

When we finally got back to our street, the first person we saw was Flor, sitting on her front porch.

"Where were you? Your parents are looking for you everywhere."

"It's a long story," I said.

We went around the back of our house. I could see my parents at the far end of the alley.

And they weren't calling cat names. They were calling our names!

FIVE
Shipwrecked in a car

All week, it had been hot enough to fry an egg on the sidewalk. At least, that's what they were saying on the radio. Miro went down to the basement, stretched out as far as he could on the cool cement floor and spent the day sleeping. On the news, there were warnings about dangerously high heat and humidity levels.

We were experiencing the Heat Wave of the Century.

The news announcers kept telling us to drink lots of liquids, stay in the shade and, above all, not lose our cool.

But some people did lose their cool. My mother,

for example. When she opened the front door on the eighth day of the heat wave, there was a squirrel on the doormat, munching away, with yellow petals all around it.

The squirrel had beheaded every one of her sunflowers.

My mother saw red, which is definitely not a cool color. She started throwing shoes at the squirrel. And not just any shoes — my baseball cleats. She missed by a mile, and knocked over two of her geraniums.

Meanwhile, the squirrel ran off with the sunflower in its mouth. I think it was chuckling.

"Where's Miro when we need him?"

"Downstairs," Max told her, "keeping cool."

I walked out to the sidewalk to pick up my shoes. Just then, wouldn't you know it, Jean-Marie came past on his bike.

"Hey, Charlie," he called in his irritating voice. "You're supposed to throw the ball, not your shoe."

The squirrels had been up to no good in the backyard, too. A couple of Dad's ripe red tomatoes were lying on the ground. A squirrel had pulled them off the plant, taken one small bite out of each, then left them lying in the dirt. In the tree above our heads, the squirrels were making laughing noises.

"They're just rats," my mother said. She had

grabbed one of my shoes again. I hoped she wouldn't throw it. "Rats with bushy tails."

"I've got an idea," Max announced, and he ran into the house.

I thought he was going to wake up Miro. Instead, he came back with his Super Soaker water gun — the small one because he hadn't made any money to buy the giant size. He filled it at the outdoor faucet and plopped down in a lawn chair by the tomatoes.

"This is my new summer job," he announced. "I'll squirt those pests if they try to come back."

Sure enough, Jean-Marie came walking down the alley. Max ran in a crouch like a soldier to the bushes near the back fence, and when Jean-Marie

passed by, he popped up and sprayed him in the ear. Jean-Marie yelled in surprise, and Max got him in the mouth. Jean-Marie jumped over the fence after him, and the chase was on.

A little later, my mother came down to the basement where I was stretched out on Miro's favorite scratching couch, reading.

"It's way too hot to work," she decided. "How about we all cool off at the pool? Go find Max."

We weren't the only ones trying to cool off. The public pool was so packed you could hardly see the water. We managed to find a small spot in the shade to spread out our towels. Max immediately ran to the edge of the pool ("No running!" the lifeguard shouted) and launched himself in ("No diving!"). Actually, he belly-flopped in. He's the king of belly-flops. People put their hands over their eyes when he belly-flops because it's too painful to watch.

I swam to the other end of the pool and pretended I didn't know him. I saw Flor sitting by herself, reading. I went over and asked what book it was.

"*Luces del Norte.*" She held up the book. I knew the picture on the cover. It was *The Golden Compass*, but in Spanish. I love that book! I've read it two times.

Flor decided to come in swimming with me, but pretty soon Max showed up and started splashing water at Jean-Marie. ("No water-fights!" the lifeguard called.)

When our fingers and toes were as wrinkled as prunes, my mother suggested we cool off a little more with some Popsicles.

She invited Flor to come along. And since parents always ask questions, and since my mother is really nosy, I found out that Flor came from Barcelona with her mother and father, who were going to teach at the university here.

We picked out our Popsicles. I took grape, and Flor took orange, because that was her favorite color. Max always chooses light blue, which is weird, because there aren't any light blue fruits.

"Sky flavor," he said.

On the way back from the store, Flor and I licked our Popsicles at a hundred miles an hour. Still, by the time we got to my house, one minute away, they were melting all over our hands.

By the middle of the afternoon, my father came home.

"I give up," he said. "No one can work in this heat."

"We could go pick up my baseball glove," I reminded him for the fiftieth time that week.

Just then, thunder growled in the distance. In the west, enormous black clouds were piling up, one on top of the other.

"I don't think you're going to play this evening."

"But I bet there's just enough time for you to cut the grass," Mom said to Dad.

Suddenly, he decided that driving me to the used sports-equipment store was a good idea. The store was the only place where you could get your baseball glove restrung. An old glove is always better than a new one, because the leather is soft and worked in.

By the time we reached the store, it was raining hard. At first it came straight down, as if someone had turned on a faucet. The drops were as big as dinner plates. As we ran into the store, the wind started to blow.

Inside, I inspected my glove. The webbing had been replaced, and there were new leather strings all across the top. A masterpiece!

"I did the work myself," the man behind the counter said. "But I don't think you'll be playing today. They say the storm is going to be bad."

We got soaked just running back to the car. The rain fell so hard it came right through the umbrella, so I put my glove under my shirt to protect it.

We started driving back to the house. Giant gusts of wind were bending the trees in all directions. Lightning struck very close by. There was an explosion and the sky lit up yellow for a second, then went black.

"A transformer got hit," my father explained.

The street had filled with water and turned into a river. Big tree branches were floating past. I turned on the car radio.

"Heavy rains, high winds, hail, lightning, tornado warnings," the announcer said. He sounded really happy.

"Looks like the weatherman got it right," my father said. "For once."

There was too much static on the radio from the lightning, so I turned it off as we lined up with the other cars to turn onto the ramp to the Decarie Expressway.

The expressway isn't exactly underground, but it is below ground level, and open above, not like a tunnel. Which meant we could feel the rain beating down on us. The car roof sounded like a set of drums in a heavy metal band.

The rain was so hard I could see the reflection of our headlights in it. My father put the wipers on high, but that only made things worse. We moved forward slowly, with cars on both sides crawling along next to us.

"This water's pretty deep," my father said, trying to sound like he drove through rivers every day.

We were trapped on the expressway, since the next exit was a long way off. A car passed us, going fast, sending waves splashing against our doors.

"What does he think he's driving? A speedboat?"

I tried to make a joke so my father would re-lax. His forehead was almost touching the inside of the windshield, and he kept wiping the steamed-up window. We were following the taillights of the car ahead of us.

All of a sudden they glowed red, and the car stopped. We had to stop, too.

"What's he doing that for? Why's he stopping?"

Something had happened up ahead. Maybe the guy who thought he was driving a speedboat caused an accident, or got stuck in the deep water. We couldn't see a thing.

Lightning flashed all around us, and the thunder exploded right above our heads. If lightning strikes your car, you're safe because the rubber tires don't conduct electricity. I learned that in science class. But the teacher never said anything about what happens if the rubber tires are sitting in water which, as everyone knows, is an excellent conductor. I decided I didn't want to find out.

"What's that sound?" my father asked.

There was so much noise all at the same time. The lightning was sizzling, the thunder crashing, the hail pounding the roof of the car, the water sloshing...

Sloshing?

I looked down at my feet. Water was coming into the car from underneath.

"Dad." I pointed, and he looked down.

"We'd better get out of here. If the water gets much higher, the engine will stall."

He turned the wheel and pulled onto the shoulder, where normally you weren't allowed to drive. But this was definitely not a normal day.

Static or not, I put on the radio.

"Cars are stalled on the Decarie Expressway," the announcer was saying. "Apparently the water is rising to dangerous levels there."

"I could have told you that," my father said.

"At least they know we're here."

I started thinking about all the movies I'd seen where cars fall into the water. How does the hero escape? How long will a car float? Are you supposed to open the windows or keep them closed? Should we stay in the car or climb out and sit on the roof? Can you swim in a flooded expressway?

Then I remembered my father could hardly swim at all. Would I have to save him?

He rolled down the window and tried to look outside. He got a face full of rain.

"Charlie, we'd better make a plan. If the water keeps rising, we'll have to abandon the car. We'll push open the doors. If the water's too deep or the current is too strong, we'll have to get up on the roof. Does that sound all right with you?"

"Sure."

"And remember to keep your glove dry!"

When things get really bad, at least my father keeps his sense of humor.

All of a sudden, the hail that had been pounding on the car stopped. That turned out to be a good thing, because we could hear a much more important sound: someone shouting at us from a bullhorn.

I opened my window a little and got slapped in the face by a wave. I wiped the water out of my eyes and shielded them with my hand.

"A ladder is coming down the side of the wall," I said.

Through the roar of the storm, we heard a voice over the bullhorn.

"Stay in your cars. Don't panic. We're coming to get you."

At least I think that's what the voice said. It could have been saying, "Say your prayers, we're going to forget you." With the crash of the thunder and the drumming rain, it was hard to tell.

The feet of a ladder were coming down the wall right next to our car. They disappeared into the water and settled on the road underneath.

A couple of seconds later, a fireman appeared on the ladder. He was wearing a yellow raincoat and hat and thigh-high rubber boots.

I waved my hand out the window.

"You're all right in there?"

"A little wet," I called back.

"Me, too. Now listen. Shut off the engine and leave the key in the ignition. If you can't get out the door, use the window. I'll help you."

"Leave the key?" my father shouted back. "What if someone tries to steal the car?"

"Sir, if someone can steal your car on a day like this, you should let him have it!"

I pushed against the car door, but the water pushed back harder. I rolled the window all the way down and crawled through it with my glove tucked under my shirt. I'd seen people do that in the movies. The fireman grabbed my shoulders, and the next thing I knew I was clinging to the ladder, completely soaked but in no danger of drowning.

"Can you climb the ladder by yourself?" the fireman asked.

"Sure!"

I climbed a few rungs, then looked down to see if my father would get out.

For a moment nothing happened. What was he going to do? Stay in the car? Did he really think someone would try to steal it?

Then I remembered that he didn't like water.

The next thing I knew, he was wriggling out the car window. He was wearing his shoes tied around his neck, and his pants were rolled up to his knees. I don't know why he bothered, since the water was way deeper than that. The fireman helped him onto the ladder, and he started climbing.

At the very top, another fireman was waiting to help me. I turned back and saw my father clinging to the ladder. He had stopped moving, and he looked frozen.

"Don't look down!" I yelled to him.

He looked up and smiled, a little embarrassed. That's how I found out that not only doesn't he like water, but he's afraid of heights, too.

The fireman tapped me on the shoulder and pointed to a bus. COMMAND CENTRAL, it said on the side. I didn't go in right away. Since I was already as wet as a drowned rat, I waited for my father.

All along the top of the wall, people were climbing off ladders in the glare of flashing lights from the fire trucks. Vans from all the television stations were there, with reporters standing under two umbrellas each.

It was a major operation, and I was right in the middle of it!

"Come on, Charlie, you'll get wet!"

My father, Captain Obvious, hadn't noticed we were both already soaking.

We ran for the Command Central bus. Inside, a man dressed like an army general was handing out blankets and coffee and hot chocolate to the people who had been rescued. A lot of them sounded very upset, even though they were in the middle of a big adventure, and they weren't in any danger. Some were crying about their cars getting ruined. Others were mad because they were late for a meeting. Nearly all of them had cellphones, and they were going on and on about how terrible the storm was, as if whoever was on the other end of the line couldn't look out the window and see for themselves.

Of course, we couldn't call anyone because we didn't have a cellphone. By the time my parents are ready to get one, people will probably have phones built into their ears.

"When can I get my car back?" my father asked the man in the uniform.

The man looked at my father as if he'd just asked the world's stupidest question.

"When the expressway's reopened, sir."

"When do you think that will be?"

"Your guess is as good as mine. It has to stop raining, which should happen pretty soon according to the radar. Then the road has to drain. No telling how long that will take. But we've arranged alternative means of transportation."

Alternative means of transportation. Why couldn't these guys talk like normal people?

"What does that mean?" I asked.

"Someone will drive you home."

Now that was more like it!

My father gave the man his name, phone number and our license plate number. Then the man started dividing the stranded people into groups, according to our neighborhoods. When it was our turn to leave, a policeman wearing rubber boots splashed into Command Central.

"Put these on," he told my father and me, handing us each a green garbage bag.

"We're already pretty wet," I told him.

"Right. But the inside of my car isn't."

I'd never ridden in a police car before. Maybe everyone would think we had been arrested. We drove past the subway station in the pouring rain. Hundreds of people were standing around in front of it.

"Subway's flooded," the policeman said. "Quite the afternoon."

On the way to our house, I saw people in bathing suits splashing through the flooded streets. In some places, water was shooting into the air where man-hole covers had blown off. Trees had fallen on cars and crushed them flat as pancakes.

We finally reached our street. An enormous tree branch was blocking it.

"We'll get out here," my father said, and we both thanked the policeman.

We had to climb over the branch to get to our house. The electricity was off everywhere, but at least our house was still standing. We went inside to tell my mother and Max the whole story. Of course, my father made it sound like he was the hero who had saved us from the flood.

I didn't say anything. I guess when you're scared of something, you want to keep it to yourself.

"You've got to see this, Charlie," Max interrupted.

He led me halfway downstairs. The basement was full of brown muddy water.

"Look!" Max said, very excited. "A flood."

"Really? And here I thought it was our new indoor swimming pool."

In the middle of the shallow lake that used to be our basement, Miro was shipwrecked on top of his couch. He was the Robinson Crusoe of cats.

Suddenly we heard a gurgling sound, and the water started to disappear, just like in a bathtub. Five minutes later, it had gone down the drain in the basement floor, leaving a slimy coat of mud on everything.

The storm of the century was over.

SIX
Dog days

The dog days of summer wore on. That's an expression my dad uses. And speaking of dogs, I decided to get serious again about finding a job before summer ended. I checked out the *Job Opportunities* section in the neighborhood newspaper… and found just what I was looking for.

Wanted. Reliable, strong, experienced dog-walker for our dog Tiny. Call (514) 555-DOGS.

I could do that. I was reliable. I was strong. I didn't have much experience, but how hard could it be? You put the dog on the leash, and then you walk it!

I called the owner. He didn't seem to mind that

I didn't have a dog myself. I told him I had a lot of experience taking care of my little brother, and he laughed.

But when the owner, a huge guy with a bald head and an earring, opened the door of his apartment, I found myself face to face with Tiny: a giant, drooling Great Dane.

The dog looked me in the eye. He was as tall as I was. He grinned. He was probably thinking, "Oh, boy, am I going to have fun with this skinny kid!"

Tiny's owner was pretty big, too. He didn't drool, but he did tower over his dog.

I looked up, swallowed hard and told a little white lie.

"Actually, I came to tell you I can't take the job.

I have to take care of my brother instead. Thanks anyway!"

"Well, family is important."

The man shook my hand, just about breaking all the bones in my fingers. Tiny looked disappointed.

At least I had some experience now, and knew what questions to ask. So when I called the second dog-walker ad, the first thing I did was ask the owner, Mrs. Skilos, what kind of dog she had.

"Oh, I have a dear little dog," she said. She was a very old lady, judging from her creaky voice. "She's a… I don't remember, but she's very sweet, yes, she is."

The lady sounded a little uncertain, but as long as the dog was small, I was ready to take my chances.

As I left the house, Max came barreling toward me.

"Where are you going? What are you doing? Can I come?"

I sighed. I wanted to do something by myself for once.

"I think Mom's calling you," I told him. "Can't you hear her? She's baking chocolate chip cookies and she needs you to lick the spoon." Max stopped dead in his tracks, turned and rushed back into the house.

Talk about little white lies. That was a good one!

As soon as the door slammed shut, I sprinted down the alley and dashed across the street. By the time Max found out that Mom hadn't called him and wasn't baking cookies and didn't have any spoons that needed licking, I would be long gone.

On the next street over, I rang the doorbell of an old rundown house with a porch full of peeling paint and a front lawn that badly needed a haircut. I must have waited five minutes. Then I heard shuffling feet, and the door opened slowly.

A very small, very wrinkled old lady peered out. "Yes?" she asked.

"Mrs. Skilos?" I said. "I'm here for the dog-walking job. I just spoke to you on the phone."

Mrs. Skilos looked at me for a few seconds. Then she smiled. At least, I think she was smiling. It was a little hard to tell with all her wrinkles.

"Oh, yes, of course! How lovely of you to have come. Now, would you like to meet my dogs?"

Dogs? With an "s"?

Sure enough, three small yappy dogs with squashed-in noses came trotting onto the porch and immediately started licking my ankles.

"See?" said Mrs. Skilos in her wavery voice. "They like you already. Now, that's Baby," she said, pointing to one of the dogs. "And that's Sweetie... No, no, the other one is Sweetie, and this one... this is Sugar. At least, I think so."

She turned to me as if I could help out with their names. She really was confused, and I couldn't blame her. The dogs all looked the same: dustballs with squashed-in noses.

Mrs. Skilos reminded me of my grandmother, who had started to forget things. Sometimes she got this trembly, cloudy look, as if she were in another world.

I felt sorry for Mrs. Skilos.

"Do you want me to walk your dogs now?" I asked.

"Yes, please!" Mrs. Skilos told me. Then she closed the door in my face.

The dogs turned circles around my feet, excited to be sniffing a new person's shoes. I rang the bell again and the door opened slowly.

"Yes?" Mrs. Skilos said. Then she saw the dogs. "Oh! What beautiful dogs! They look just like mine."

"That's because they *are* your dogs. And if I'm going to walk them, I'll need their leashes."

I was starting to think this dog-walking business was not going to work out.

"Lashes?" she asked, blinking her eyes rapidly. "Eyelashes?"

"No, leashes. Dog leashes."

Then suddenly, just like that, she understood perfectly. She turned and took three leashes from a hook just inside her door.

"Here they are, young man. Be careful with my sweeties, they're very precious to me. I expect you back in exactly one hour."

Then she closed the door again. I reached down and tied the leashes to the dogs' collars and set off on my first official summer job.

I don't know if you have ever gone fishing, but imagine you're fishing with three different rods and you catch three different fish at the same time. The lines get all tangled up because the three fish are pulling in three different directions at once.

Well, that's exactly what it was like to walk Baby, Sweetie and Sugar — the furry triplets. They pulled this way and that. Then one would stop to pee and the other two would bump headlong into it, and all three would start squealing and fighting.

Finally they agreed on one thing. They all collapsed on the sidewalk together, panting in the dog-day heat, and they refused to move another inch.

I kneeled down, talked into their furry ears, petted and encouraged them, but they wouldn't listen.

Dog-walking is not as easy as it sounds, I can tell you that! Especially when all three decided to do their business at the same time. And I had only one small plastic bag for three dogs. I picked up one pile of dog business, folded the bag, then picked up another pile… I think you get the picture. Once I finished picking up after all of them, I couldn't wait to get to the nearest trash can.

Finally we reached the dog park. I figured it would be a good idea to let the furry triplets run free and get some exercise. But this wasn't my day for brilliant ideas.

Have you ever noticed how dogs always look like their owners? Or maybe it's the owners who look like their dogs.

That was convenient, in a way. In the dog park where all the dogs ran free, I could tell which dog belonged to which person.

For instance, the huge Saint Bernard belonged to the large man with the bushy brown beard. The Chihuahua belonged to the nervous, skinny little woman who couldn't sit still. The cocker spaniel had his owner's sad brown eyes and long ears, and so on.

That's how everyone in the dog park knew the furry triplets didn't belong to me, since I didn't have a wrinkled face and a squashed-in nose. And they could also tell because I had no control over them. As soon as I let the dogs free, they went totally berserk!

First they tried to attack the Saint Bernard, but he just stared at them as if they were ants running around his feet. When that didn't work, the furry triplets peed on his owner's shoes. Then they started turning circles around the Chihuahua until the poor dog was about to have a heart attack.

I called the furry triplets. I scolded them. I ran after them and tried to catch them. But they stayed just out of reach, yipping and yapping their heads off.

Finally, the Saint Bernard's owner scooped up all three of them in one huge hand and delivered them to me.

"First time you've walked these dogs?" he asked. "Maybe you should keep them on a leash. They've obviously figured out that you're an amateur." The man gave a big laugh and walked away with his Saint Bernard trotting at his heel. His dog had probably gone to obedience school and graduated with straight As.

Not Baby, Sweetie and Sugar. I was red with embarrassment as I snapped the leashes back onto the three dustballs and led them out of the park.

I wasn't just embarrassed. I was exhausted. I dragged them over to Beaubien Park so I could sit on a bench in the shade for a while. This time I kept them on their leashes.

For a while, everything was quiet. There was a nice breeze in the shade and I could hear the fountain splashing in the middle of the park. Little kids learning how to rollerskate wobbled by. Finally, I started to relax.

My arm was almost pulled out of its socket by all three dogs making a desperate lunge at the same time. The dustballs had spotted a squirrel! They ripped the leashes from my hand and started chasing the squirrel through the park, around and around in circles, barking their heads off.

Then the squirrel leapt onto the edge of the fountain and began laughing as Baby, Sweetie and Sugar dived into the water after it.

I was up to my knees in the fountain, fishing

out one wet dustball after another, when I heard a girl's voice.

"Are you washing those dogs, or are they washing you?"

I turned around. There was Flor, trying her best not to laugh. I told her about my dog-walking job.

"That sounds like a good one," she said. "But maybe you could use some help."

First I got the dogs out of the fountain. By then they had forgotten all about the squirrel. Flor helped me untangle the leashes and sort out the dogs. After that, we set off for Mrs. Skilos' house.

Flor seemed to know how to control the dogs. She could make them stop and wait at the curb before we crossed a street, or walk in a straight line so their leashes wouldn't get tangled.

"Where did you learn so much about dogs?" I asked her.

"I used to have a dog when I lived in Spain. But he died a year ago." Her face turned sad for a moment. I understood why she was so careful with her cat Blanquita.

When Mrs. Skilos opened the door and saw her dogs, she was overjoyed.

"I thought I'd lost my sweeties," she said as she kissed each dog. "I was looking everywhere for them."

She leaned over and kissed us, too, on both cheeks.

"Thank you both so much!"

Then she dug into her apron pockets and gave us each two dollars for "finding" her dogs.

The first thing Flor and I did was go down to the corner store and buy ice cream cones. That was the end of my dog-walking career. I decided I'd better quit while I was ahead.

That evening, we had dinner in the backyard, at the picnic table that still smelled a bit like skunk. I told my parents the whole story about Mrs. Skilos. Max was still mad about me tricking him with the cookies, and he kept saying I should have taken him along.

The furry triplets *and* my brother? That would have been a bigger disaster!

My mother was worried about Mrs. Skilos.

"It sounds like she's very much alone, and a little mixed up. She reminds me of my mother. I think we should go visit her. I bet we can help out."

Maybe that would be my new summer job. Looking after Mrs. Skilos. It would probably be easier than taking care of her dogs.

One evening at dinner, my mother announced, "We have a great idea for you guys…"

What had my parents come up with this time? Golf lessons? Badminton camp? They should have figured out by now that we're not an organized kind of family.

But this time they surprised me.

"Fred and Marie could use some help on their farm," my father said.

Now that was more like it! Fred and Marie are friends of my parents, and they're real farmers. They have miles and miles of apple orchards, not very far from Montreal. We get to do all kinds of things there we can't do in the city, like drive Fred's tractor, and go swimming in his pond, and eat all the apples we want.

"And we thought, if you don't mind, that you could go by yourselves…"

"Because we have a lot of work to do…"

"You could take the bus, and they'll be waiting for you…"

"What do you say?"

Did my parents actually think we'd refuse?

The next day, our parents got ready to drive us down to the bus station. This time, my mother was at the wheel.

She was just learning how to drive. She says it's a family tradition. Her mother never learned to drive, and her grandmother never drove, either. Of course, there weren't any cars back then.

Mom finally decided to take driving lessons, and she was supposed to practice as often as possible.

"You need to try some city driving," my father told her, settling in on the passenger side. "We'll take Park Avenue."

"Park Avenue is a madhouse," my mother answered. "I never ride my bike on that street."

"We're not riding your bike. We're driving. Driving is easy."

"If it was easy, I would have learned by now."

My mother put the car in Drive and it jumped forward. Then she stepped on the brake hard. I tightened my seatbelt.

"Relax," my father told her.

"I'd relax if you'd stop telling me to relax."

Away we went.

Mom was right. Park Avenue was a madhouse. The city was tearing up the street to put in a new sewer system. People riding bikes and pushing strollers and grocery carts had to steer around gigantic holes and those striped cones that look like clown hats.

As we crawled along the street at zero miles an hour, my father kept giving my mother advice.

"Line up the edge of the left front fender with the center line of the road."

"There is no center line," my mother pointed out.

"Adjust your mirrors."

"I already have."

"Your eyes should sweep the road in front of you. Don't stare at one fixed point."

I caught my mother's expression in the rear-view mirror. She looked like she was going to take a bite out of my father.

We crept along Park Avenue. She must have thought that the slower she drove, the safer she would be. Two bicycle riders passed us, one on either side.

"Pedal faster!" one of them shouted.

Instead, she hit the brakes. The traffic light in front of us turned red.

Immediately, a gang of squeegee kids appeared out of nowhere to wash our windshield.

"Run the windshield wipers, quick," my father told her.

"Why? It's not raining."

"It's to keep them from…"

But it was too late. The squeegees were already squirting soapy water on the windshield and wiping it dry. Now that's a summer job I wouldn't want!

My mother rummaged through her purse, looking for money. Unfortunately, she couldn't find any.

Meanwhile, the light changed to green.

A taxi squeezed past us.

"Hey, lady! This is no place for a nap!" the driver called.

I slumped down in my seat and tried to act invisible.

Finally, my mother found a quarter and gave it to the squeegee kids. They didn't look too impressed.

The light turned green a second time but we still didn't move. That's because people kept crossing against the light, and my mother believes that pedestrians have the right of way — no matter what. Drivers were honking like mad behind us.

"Hurry up!" my father said. "We're going to miss the bus."

"That does it! I quit!"

My mother jumped out of the car, walked around to the passenger side and opened the door. My father took the hint. He got out and changed places with my mother.

We made it to the bus station in plenty of time, by the way.

Our parents insisted on waiting with us until the bus left. They used the time to give us advice. Don't forget your bags, don't bother the driver, sit still during the trip... Then they had to make a big embarrassing scene, kissing us as we were trying to get on board, right in front of the passengers and the driver. Afterwards they stood there, waving like crazy, until the bus pulled away.

"First trip away from home?" the driver laughed.

The bus drove through downtown Montreal, then over the Champlain Bridge. Pretty soon we were surrounded by cornfields and cows. I switched on my iPod. Nature always looks better if you have the right tunes. Apart from one crying baby and the bus driver, everyone seemed to be sleeping, Max included. He was snoring like an old vacuum cleaner.

Then, all of a sudden, everything changed.

The engine started coughing like it had a bad cold, and I felt the bus slowing down. The next thing I knew, the driver was steering onto the edge of the highway. He was using some words I can't repeat here.

After that, he got on the loudspeaker.

"Sorry, folks, but we have some temporary technical issues."

He could have told us the bus had broken down, but that would have been too simple.

Everybody started talking at once. Even Max woke up.

"What do we do now?"

"Go get some fresh air," I told him. "At least we're not in an airplane."

We all filed out of the bus. The driver was standing on the edge of the road, talking on his cellphone and waving his arms in the air.

"No!" I heard him yell. "I don't want a mechanic. I want another bus!"

I agreed with him one hundred percent.

Meanwhile, the passengers were walking up and down the side of the road, complaining to each other. They couldn't complain to the driver, because he was too busy complaining to someone else.

Max and I slipped down the side of the ditch, then hopped across it. On the other side was a field, and around it ran a wire fence to keep the cows in. Black cows with big white patches on their sides like clouds.

Max squeezed between the wires and went into the field.

"Watch out for the bulls!" I called. "They'll chase you!"

"They're not bulls. They're cows. And cows don't chase people."

"Here they come!"

But the cows just looked up from their chewing and stared at Max. Of course he had to do his famous cow imitation. The cows seemed to like that. They all mooed back.

"I told you cows don't chase people," he said. "I bet I could even pet one."

He started to wander into the field.

"All right," I told him. "But watch out for the —"

"Oh, yuck!"

" — cow-pies!"

Wouldn't you know it? Max stepped in a very large, very fresh cow-pie.

I looked across the field at the cows. I think they were laughing.

Max started doing a little dance, trying to rub the bottom and the sides of his shoe on the grass. That was quite the show!

A horn honked on the road behind us. The replacement bus pulled up, and all the passengers started cheering.

Max slipped back under the fence. I couldn't help mooing, just a little.

"Stop that!" he said.

Then he ran for the bus.

I waited my turn with all the other passengers who were still complaining about how they were going to be late getting to their stop. I found my seat, but Max wasn't there. I wasn't too surprised. He was probably trying to clean his shoes in the toilet.

The engine roared, and we were back on the road again.

About fifteen minutes later, the driver got a call on his cellphone. The next thing I knew, he was slowing down, even though we were still in the middle of the countryside. He parked by the side of the road and got to his feet. Then he walked down the aisle with heavy steps.

He stopped in front of me. He looked pretty irritated.

"Did you lose your brother, by any chance?" he asked.

"Uh, not that I know of. Let me go look."

With all the passengers staring, I rushed down the aisle to the back of the bus and knocked on the door to the toilet.

"Hey, Max!"

No answer. I knocked again. You could never tell with Max. Maybe he was still mad at my cow jokes.

Finally, I opened the door. He wasn't there.

It seemed to take forever to walk back to my seat. All the passengers were staring at me, looking annoyed. The driver stood, tapping his foot.

"I guess I did lose him," I said.

"That's what I thought," the driver said. Then he sat down behind the wheel again.

He turned the bus around. Pretty soon we were driving back the way we came. I slipped down in my seat so no one could see me.

When it's not my parents embarrassing me, it's Max!

A few minutes later, we stopped next to our old bus. The biggest tow truck I had ever seen was slowly lifting the front of it into the air, lights flashing on all sides. That was pretty impressive, but I still didn't see Max.

Then, all of a sudden, there he was. I couldn't believe it! He was sitting inside the bus in the driver's seat, with both hands on the big steering wheel. He was pretending to drive, as happy as could be.

"I guess we know what he wants to be when he grows up," the driver said, shaking his head. "We'd better get him out of there before he gets towed away."

The tow truck lowered him back to the ground, and the passengers burst into applause. Max thought they were applauding him, and he gave them a big smile and bowed. But I knew better. They were cheering because finally, just maybe, they would get to their destination.

"*Terminus!* Granby Station!"

I must have fallen asleep, because all of a sudden we were in a town, pulling into the bus station. Everyone stood up and grabbed their bags, in a big hurry to get off.

I looked out the window. It was strange. We were supposed to be at the stop near Fred's farm, not in another city.

"End of the line!" the driver shouted. "Everybody off!"

A little dazed, Max and I climbed out of the bus.

"Is this Abbotsford?" I asked the driver.

"Granby! The end of the line."

"But we were supposed to go to Abbotsford."

"That's the milk run, the local. Your parents must have put you on the wrong bus. With you kids, somehow I'm not surprised."

I couldn't believe it. After all their warnings and advice, my parents had managed to make the worst possible mistake!

"Now what?" Max said.

"We have to get a hold of Fred and Marie."

We wandered out of the station. I had Fred and Marie's phone number, but I couldn't find a pay phone. And I didn't know how much the call would cost, because I didn't know how far Granby was from Abbotsford.

Otherwise, everything was perfectly fine.

The town of Granby didn't have much going for it. There was hardly anyone on the main street, and all the stores looked closed.

Then I heard a tremendous roar, as if a low-flying jet was buzzing the town. The next minute a long line of motorcycles came by, making as much noise as possible. It was pretty cool.

Max and I stared at them through a tornado of dust and smoke. No sooner did those riders disappear than another wave came down the street. Some wore army helmets with spikes on top. Others wore dark visors over their faces, like Darth Vader.

We walked to the next corner. There were no pay phones anywhere. Maybe no one ever needed to call anyone in Granby.

While I was searching for a phone, Max spotted a row of at least a hundred motorcycles all lined up, parked very close together. He pulled me across the street to have a look.

The bikes were huge, painted black and silver, and glittering in the sun. They looked like beasts from a fantasy movie. They were so shiny and polished that you almost had to wear sunglasses to look at them.

Some had gas tanks that were like mirrors. You could see your reflection in them, and the frames were all made of chrome. Some had little trailers with flame decals, or sidecars where passengers could ride. Others had their frames fixed in a special way so the front tires were far ahead of the rest of the bike.

Max stuck his face very close to the gas tank of one of the motorcycles. The tank was like one of those curved mirrors in the funhouse at the carnival — the kind that make you look all crazy. Max started making funny faces, bugging out his eyes and doing his fish imitation.

"What are you doing, kid? I spent all morning shining my machine!"

Max jumped a foot in the air. I turned around.

In front of me stood a greasy, dirty version of Santa Claus — in the middle of summer. The man had a huge beer belly, long white hair and a yellowish beard. He was wearing jeans that looked as though they had been washed in motor oil. His T-shirt had the sleeves ripped off so you could see his fading tattoos.

I grabbed Max and we stepped back. The man towered over us.

"Sorry," I said. "My little brother likes to clown around."

The man grunted and walked over to his motorcycle. With the tail of his T-shirt, he polished his gas tank where Max had breathed on it.

One by one, more enormous, white-haired, white-bearded guys slowly walked out of a building. Maybe it was their clubhouse.

No one was exactly saying ho-ho-ho. It was pretty scary being surrounded by very dirty Santas, complete with tattoos, on a sidewalk in a strange town. Especially when you were lost.

"Your little brother, huh?" the man asked.

"Yes, sir."

"Sir? You're very polite."

"Yes, sir."

"I like polite kids."

I figured I'd said "Yes, sir" enough times. So I didn't say anything at all.

"And what are two polite kids like you doing in Granby on a day like this?"

It was a very good question.

"Well, you see, we're lost, sort of. We got on the wrong bus and ended up here. I was looking for a pay phone to call the people who are supposed to meet us."

He squinted at me, as if my story was a little too complicated to be true. Then he laughed. A loud laugh that was a little greasy, just like his jeans. He pointed to the street corner.

"Son, do you see a pay phone down there?"

"No, sir."

He laughed and pointed to the next corner.

"Do you see a pay phone up there?"

"No, sir."

"Well, kid, there used to be two perfectly good pay phones on both corners. Then the phone company came and took them out. You can't call any-

one anymore unless you have a cellphone. If you
ask me, that's a crime."

"I agree."

"Where did you say you boys were headed?"

"Abbotsford."

"No kidding! Who do you know in Abbotsford?
I went to high school there."

"Fred and Marie. You wouldn't — "

"Fred? Freddie Fish? You don't say!"

The man slapped himself so hard on the forehead I was afraid he'd knock himself out. Then
he pulled a cellphone from his pocket and started
punching numbers.

"Fred Fish? Hey, Bob here… Yeah, yeah, Greasy
Bob, very funny. Long time no see… Are you miss-
ing a couple of polite little kids by any chance…?
Not *that* polite?"

The two of them talked for a while. Then Greasy
Bob handed me the phone. It was pretty greasy, too.

I heard Fred's voice. "So you met my old friend
Bob, have you, Charlie? What a stroke of luck! We
were starting to get worried. He's going to give you
a lift over to Abbotsford. See you soon!"

He hung up. Amazing! The one person we met
in Granby was a high-school friend of Fred's.

"Max," I said, "we're going for a ride."

Bob opened a compartment at the back of the
sidecar and took out two helmets.

"Here, these'll fit. My grandkids wear them when we go riding."

Max didn't like his helmet because it was bright pink, but he strapped it on anyway. The helmets had visors to protect our eyes from the wind and the bugs.

We climbed into the sidecar. There was just enough room. Good thing Max didn't have to sit on my lap. That would have ruined the trip.

Bob put on his jean jacket and helmet and hopped on the motorcycle. *Granddads on Wheels* was written on the back of his jacket, with the picture of an old guy on a bike. Then he started up his engine and revved it, making about as much noise as an explosion in a firecracker factory.

"Ready, boys?"

We glided down the main street of Granby. Bob made such a racket, he sounded like ten motorcycles. Everyone stopped and watched as we went by. I guess it wasn't every day that they saw a couple of kids wearing fluorescent helmets with tinted visors riding in a sidecar.

A few minutes later, we were out in the country, zipping along the narrow roads. It was like riding a rollercoaster. Fields flashed by with black-and-white blurs that were cows. Flocks of birds rose up in front of us.

I felt like I was traveling at the speed of light.

I wanted the ride to last forever.

Unfortunately, Abbotsford isn't very far from Granby. Not nearly far enough.

We turned off the highway and onto Fish Road, to Fred and Marie's place. Imagine having the road where you live named after you! The next minute we made our grand entrance into the front yard of the apple farm. Bob managed to rev his engine so it sounded like gunshots, and we came to a stop in a swirling cloud of dust.

Fred and Marie appeared through the cloud, coughing and waving their hands in front of their faces. Fred slapped Greasy Bob on the back as Marie pulled us from the sidecar and hugged us.

"You boys are so brave! I'd be afraid to ride in one of those things."

"What happened to you guys?" Fred asked.

"We got on the wrong bus," Max explained.

"Actually, our parents put us on the wrong bus," I said.

Bob patted me on the top of the head. I thought my neck would break.

"These kids picked the best weekend of the year to get stuck in Granby. The international biker festival. I'm afraid I've got to get back, though. My pals are waiting for me."

He and Fred shook hands again. They slapped each other on the back a few more times, and Bob promised to come to the farm one day soon.

Then he rode off in a swirl of dust and enough noise to make my ears bleed.

"Okay, guys," Fred said. "Enough hanging around with bikers. It's time to work!"

I headed for the barn where Fred kept his old tractor. I climbed onto it. The keys were in the ignition, where he always left them.

I pulled out of the barn. The engine made almost as much noise as a motorcycle. The trailer loaded with apple crates bounced along the rough road.

Max ran after me, but I knew he'd never catch up.

EIGHT
Finding Bruce Lee

It was practically the end of the summer, and that meant it was my birthday. In my family, you get to do whatever *you* want on your birthday, instead of what your parents want. It's like being king for a day.

I decided that on my birthday, I was going to play baseball.

My family loves sports. My father and I are baseball maniacs. My mother plays tennis every day.

Then there's Max. He dreams of being a soccer player. "Dream" is the important word here. Sometimes, right in the middle of a game, he forgets he's supposed to be playing. That's usually when the ball comes to him.

One time his team had the ball, and someone kicked it to him. He was looking up at the sky, counting clouds. The ball hit him right on the head and bounced into the other team's goal.

He started jumping and waving his arms in the air, as if he'd actually scored the goal on purpose. Then he got down on his knees and pumped his fist.

My father, Max and I drove over to Jeanne Mance, our sports paradise. All the players say it's the most beautiful park in the world, because you have a great view of the Mountain.

Once we got there, I said to Max, "Come on, let's go get the equipment."

We ran across Mont Royal Street to the Yy convenience store. That's right. Yy.

Once I asked Grace, the owner, why it was called that.

"Why not?" she said.

The convenience store really is convenient, because that's where we store our equipment. It's always there waiting for us on the top of the fridge, from seven in the morning to eleven at night. The bats, balls, spare gloves, catcher's mask and bases are all stored in the dirtiest sports bags on earth, along with rakes and shovels to fix the field after the rain. There's even a little barbecue and a bag of charcoal.

I said *bonjour* to Grace. She was studying French and running the store at the same time. She must be pretty smart to do both things at once.

"I hope you win," she said.

"We will!"

I climbed on a chair and handed the bags down to Max. He started dragging the lightest one to the park, but in the middle of the street, he decided it was too heavy. I had to dash over and pick it up before a truck ran over it.

"More people in this park should be like you," said Ernesto, one of the players who was warming up with my father. "You are an example of civic cooperation."

The thing you have to know about Ernesto, besides that he always wears a baseball cap because he's bald, is that he was a lawyer back in his home country, in Nicaragua. When he talks, he sounds like a book.

Before I could play, I had to find a family to look after Max. Usually that's no problem. A lot of players are from the Dominican Republic, or Colombia, or Venezuela, and their families come to watch them play. They set up their barbecues behind the backstop, so there is always someone to keep an eye on Max. He can fool around with the little kids and share their picnic. As long as there's food, Max is happy. And he's learning Spanish at the same time.

My father and I were on the same team. I was playing right field, my favorite position, because I don't have the sun in my face. Our pitcher was James. He wears big sunglasses that make him look like a giant bug.

Just as James was about to throw his first pitch, an ice-cream vendor rode his tricycle right across the infield.

Everybody started yelling at him to get out of the way. I can't tell you what they said, because some of the players weren't very polite.

"Calm down, guys," James told them.

Then he bought a grape Popsicle from the ice

cream man and unwrapped it. In a few enormous bites, he ate the whole thing. Even from right field, I could see his purple mouth.

He struck out the first batter. I guess that purple Popsicle helped.

Soon we were leading by two runs. But playing in our park can be a little complicated. We aren't the only ones who think it's the most beautiful place in the world.

Two homeless people with four dogs started pushing their shopping carts across left field, where my father was playing. Then they unrolled their sleeping bags on the grass. I could see my father talking to them, pointing to the other players, so the people would understand that they were in the middle of a very important ballgame.

That didn't work. The next thing I knew, my father was pushing their carts with the sleeping bags in them at top speed, all the way to the fence that runs behind left field. The two people were running after him, as if they thought he was trying to steal their stuff.

Meanwhile, I had a different problem. No one had hit a ball to right field. I was feeling a little lonely.

Then Elvis came up to bat. That's not his real name, of course, but everyone calls him that because his black hair is perfectly combed in a swirl, just like that dead singer, Elvis Presley. I had a feeling Elvis was going to hit the ball in my direction, since he probably thought I was just a kid who couldn't catch a fly ball.

And that's exactly what happened!

He hit a lazy fly ball, very high, and I had plenty of time to get under it. With my better-than-new glove that I had saved from the flood.

But Elvis' fly ball kept curving away from me, and I kept following it into foul territory, where a line of tall elm trees stood. I was right under the ball, ready to make the catch, when — *bang!* — the ball hit one tree branch, then another, then bounced onto the sidewalk.

"Interference on the tree!" I shouted.

The ball spun into the street and hit a couple of cars. Then it started rolling down the middle of Mont Royal Street.

I saw Max making a beeline for the ball.

"I got it! I got it!" he was yelling.

My father saw him, too, all the way from left field.

"Charlie! Stop your brother!" he called.

One more time, I had to save Max from himself. And a busy street full of cars.

I ran after him, and that's when I saw the parade.

A group of very serious men in black suits and

women wearing white scarves and holding candles came marching up the street. A police car with flashing lights led the way, followed by a priest holding a banner that read *Our Lady of Fatima*. Behind him, men carried a giant statue of the Lady on their shoulders. She was covered with flowers. A marching band played sad music.

How in the world was I going to find the ball, or my brother, in the middle of a parade?

Then I spotted Max darting past the police car.

"Max!" I yelled. "Wait up!"

But all he wanted was to get his hands on the ball. He was crawling on all fours among the men in black suits. I could tell where Max was by the way the marching band guys tripped, or the way they hit sour notes as he wormed his way between their feet.

I had to wait as the parade went by with tubas and French horns playing, and the priest waving a golden jar with smoke coming out of it. The drivers who were caught in the traffic jam were honking their horns, as if the parade needed any more noise.

Meanwhile, Elvis stood with his bat on his shoulder and yelled at me to find the ball.

Suddenly Max appeared in the middle of the marching band. He was holding the ball above his head.

"I got it! I got it!"

And he ran past the lines of cars, back to the park, right by Elvis, and all the way to James, who was standing on the pitcher's mound.

Max put the ball in James' hand.

"Good work, kid," James said.

All the players applauded. Max danced around the infield as if he'd just scored the winning touchdown in the Super Bowl. He was a star — at least in his imagination.

I was out in right field in the second-to-last inning when I heard banging and grunting behind me.

"I will smite you with my well-tempered steel," someone shouted.

I turned around, wondering if Robin Hood had suddenly shown up in Montreal. There were people dressed in suits of armor, carrying swords and shields and lances in the middle of our ballpark! It didn't seem to matter to them that their armor and weapons were made out of cardboard.

"Hey, guys, can't you see there's a game going on?"

One of the cardboard knights looked at me, surprised.

"Sorry, baseball hasn't been invented yet. We're in the Middle Ages."

"You might be, but I'm not. And you're in right field."

"This is our park, too."

"It's everyone's park. But I don't know if your cardboard helmet will do much good against a fly ball."

The knights in shining cardboard wouldn't listen to me because I was a kid and they were adults, even if they didn't look very grown-up. Some of the warriors carried shields that were actually garbage can lids with lions painted on them (or maybe

they were lambs). Two girls covered in tattoos and wearing rings in their noses were trying to fight with swords that kept breaking in half. No wonder! They were made from the cardboard insides of paper towel rolls wrapped in tape.

Ernesto came running over from center field and started yelling at them in Spanish. He waved his glove in the air, shooing away the knights as if they were flies. He was pretty convincing. The knights moved to another part of the park and went on swinging their make-believe swords at each other.

Finally, the last inning rolled around and we were still ahead by two runs. Three more outs and we'd win! James was pitching really well. It must have been that purple Popsicle.

Then trouble started. My father dropped a fly ball in left field because he forgot to use both hands to catch it. The next batter got a hit. There were two outs, they had two men on base, and guess who came up to bat?

Elvis!

I could tell by the way he stood at the plate that he was going to hit the ball in my direction again.

And sure enough, he hit a soft line drive to right field.

I ran in to put myself in good position. *This one is yours*, I told myself. *It's your birthday present.*

I put my glove up to snag the ball…

All of a sudden something brown and hairy flew past my face, and the ball disappeared.

What the…?

The next thing I knew, a Doberman was racing across the field with the ball in its mouth!

The players went absolutely ape. The runners forgot to run. They stopped and yelled at the dog. They yelled at each other. It was interference on the dog. We should start the play all over again. It should be a ground-rule double.

And where was the dog? Where was the ball?

Then I heard James yelling louder than everyone else, which is saying a lot.

"Rocko, come!"

The dog appeared out of nowhere, running at top speed with the ball still in its mouth. It ran straight to James on the pitcher's mound.

"Good boy!"

The dog opened its mouth, and the ball dropped into James' mitt. He held it up for everyone to see. Dog spit dripped off it.

"Three outs! We win!"

Of course it was just a game — but there's no such thing as *just a game*. The other team's players rushed toward James and his dog, pointing at the ball, then at the dog, then at right field.

But James had it all figured out.

"Listen, guys! That's my dog. He's playing for

me. He's on my team. He caught the ball before it touched the ground. Then he brought it to me. I caught it from him. If the ball doesn't touch the ground, and if one of my players catches it, even if he's got four legs, then the batter's out. Three outs! Game over! We win!"

Our team started cheering. Max ran onto the field and tried to high-five Rocko.

The other team didn't know what to say. They grumbled, but they knew they'd lost.

Worse, they'd lost to a dog.

My reign as king for a day wasn't over yet. My grandmother had sent me money for my birthday, and I knew what I wanted to spend it on: the complete collection of Bruce Lee films.

"Let's go to Chinatown," I told my father.

"Why?" he asked.

"Chicken balls! Fried rice! Fortune cookies!" Max shouted.

"Bruce Lee movies," I told my father.

That made sense, since Bruce Lee was from Hong Kong. But I bet you didn't know he was born in the United States, and that his father was an opera singer. I wonder what he thought about his son becoming a kung fu master.

It took only five minutes to drive there, but that's when the fun began. Everyone who wasn't in

Jeanne Mance Park seemed to be in Chinatown. The sidewalks were packed and the cars were double-parked.

"Help me look for a parking space," my father said.

Max immediately started to point out all sorts of places where we *couldn't* park.

"That's a fire hydrant."

"That's for delivery trucks only."

"You need a permit there."

"That's a no parking zone."

"The guy in that car is asleep. He's not leaving."

Around and around we drove, as if a space would appear like some kind of parking miracle.

"If Mom was here," Max piped up, "she'd say that we should have ridden our bikes."

"I'm sure she would," my father growled.

We drove around the same block four or five times in the hot car that still smelled a little funny from the expressway flood.

Finally, my father stopped under the big red arch over the street that's decorated with all kinds of red dragons and Chinese characters.

"You two might as well get out," he told us. "I'll catch up to you at the store."

Max and I jumped out. The video store was on a street where no cars were allowed, so at least Max wouldn't get run over. The store wasn't hard to find.

There was a big Bruce Lee — or Lee Jun-fan in Chinese — poster in the window.

A video store in Chinatown is different from an ordinary video store. You can buy all sorts of things there besides videos: bobbing-head cats with big grins, colored fans and miniature fountains decorated with dragons and lotus blossoms. Max started playing in the miniature musical waterfall, splashing water on the piles of silk slippers.

Finally, the owner told him to stop.

"What you break, you buy," he told Max.

Everyone in the store stared at us. Sometimes I think Max tries to embarrass me on purpose. I pretended I didn't know him, and went to pay for the videos.

The next thing I knew, Max had disappeared. I wasn't surprised. If I don't pay attention to him one hundred percent of the time, he gets mad and decides to accidentally get lost.

I stepped out onto the street. I figured it wouldn't be too hard to find him. After all, he was one of the few people around who wasn't Chinese.

Well, you don't know Max. He was nowhere in sight. I looked through the window of the store next door. TRADITIONAL MEDICINES AND HERBS, the sign said. It looked like a place Max might go.

I went in and said hello to the lady behind the

counter. There were giant Max-sized sacks at the back of the store, so I headed in that direction.

I didn't find my brother, but I did see something even weirder. One of the bags was full to the brim with starfish — dried starfish. Next to that bag was another one with dried seahorses in it.

I looked up. The lady was standing next to me. "Can I help you?"

"What do you do with all these dried things?"

"For soup."

Seahorse soup? Would it taste like barnyard or fish?

The seahorses and starfish weren't the strangest things in that store. There were bags of chips, but they weren't made out of potatoes. They were made from squid — smoked squid, to be exact. There were shark fins, and sea cucumbers that didn't look anything like the cucumbers in your salad, and bags of something called dried moonfish. Not to mention the fruits and vegetables that looked like they came from outer space. They were bright pink or lime green or both, with bristles and spikes. And don't forget the bottles of seal oil, mountain dragon herbs and Chinese caterpillar fungus.

It was pretty interesting. But unfortunately, there was no sign of Max.

"Did my little brother come in here, by any

chance?" I asked the lady. "Wearing a red shirt and carrying a bag of ketchup-flavored chips?"

"No little brothers," she said. "Maybe he got shanghaied!"

She started laughing very hard, as if she had just made the funniest joke in the history of comedy. I didn't get it. What's so funny about Shanghai?

I walked out without buying any squid chips or seal oil. There was a restaurant next door. It sounded as if someone was having a big argument inside. A woman was screaming in Chinese in a very shrill voice. But no one was screaming back.

I went in. It was very dark inside, and the walls were painted red. I guess red is a lucky color if you're Chinese.

When my eyes got used to the darkness, I could see a big pool at the front of the restaurant, with a fountain in the middle and a dragon spitting water on top. The largest goldfish I had ever seen were swimming in the pool.

Then I saw the lady who was doing the yelling, and I saw the person she was yelling at.

"Don't you feed the fish!" the lady was scolding Max.

She must have figured out that Max didn't understand Chinese, because she had switched to English.

"Those aren't your fish. Those are my fish! You want to feed fish? Get your own!"

So Max was up to his old tricks again. He wasn't happy feeding Jaws to death. He was after bigger fish now.

The lady looked at me and scowled.

"You know him?" she asked.

"He's my little brother," I admitted. I really didn't have any choice.

"He was feeding my fish fortune cookies!" she said, very outraged. "Fortune cookies are no good for fish!"

"Come on, Max," I said. "Let's get out of here before she makes us do the dishes."

Very gently, I pushed Max out of the restaurant. The lady stood in front of the door and glared at us, as if she was afraid Max would sneak back in and feed her fish more cookie crumbs.

"You boys don't come back!" she ordered.

"Don't worry," I told her. "We won't."

We went and stood in front of the video store to wait for Dad.

"Happy birthday," Max said to me. He handed me a slightly crumbled fortune cookie.

I broke it open, and inside was my fortune:

YOU WILL GET A BIG SURPRISE!

What kind of surprise? A real summer job? A great adventure? Who writes these fortunes, anyway?

Just then, my father came up. He was red in the face and looked as if he'd been running.

"Parking around here is a mess. What a nightmare! Did you find what you were looking for?"

"Yes."

I started telling him about the dried seahorses and starfish.

"We'll talk in the car. I found a space, but I didn't have enough change for the parking meter."

Then he caught sight of the woman standing with her hands on her hips. She looked as though she wanted to make a Max fried rice out of my brother.

"That woman sure doesn't look very happy," my father remarked. "Did anything happen here?"

"Nope," Max and I said together.

Of course, by the time we got back to the car, a policeman was standing by the meter, writing out a parking ticket.

"Look, here we are," my father pleaded with him.

"You're too late," he said.

"But we were only gone a couple minutes," my father said. "Besides, it's my son's birthday."

"Happy birthday," the policeman said to me, as he handed my father the ticket.

When we got home, I figured I would relax with a Bruce Lee movie. My head was spinning from the hot sun at the ballpark. So far, I had done pretty much what I'd wanted for my birthday.

When I went into the kitchen to get a movie snack, I heard voices in the backyard. I looked out the window. I didn't see anyone, but our picnic table was missing.

Who would have taken it?

I decided to investigate. When I went into the yard, the alley burst into song.

"Happy birthday to you!"

All the neighbors were singing at the top of their lungs — for *my* birthday! Now that really *was* a surprise! They had set up tables in the alley for an alley picnic.

"Happy birthday, Charlie!" my mother called.

Catherine from down the block held up her fish bowl.

"Look, Jaws came, too!"

Everyone was there. I met Flor's parents. Mr. Plouffe had come. As usual, he had a piece of dried bread in his pocket. "To feed the birds," he explained. My parents had even invited Jean-Marie.

I sat down beside Flor. I told her my idea about people who look like their dogs.

"Oh," she said, "so I suppose I look like Blanquita?"

"Blanquita's a cat. People don't look like their cats, only their dogs."

Whew! That was a close call!

Then I noticed Catherine staring at her fish bowl.

"There's something different about Jaws. But I don't know what. I'm worried."

"He's smiling," said Max. "It's because it's Charlie's birthday."

"He probably likes to get a little fresh air once in a while," I added. "Hey, here comes the food!"

But Catherine went on staring at her fish even after the hamburgers arrived.

"Sorry, Flor, I'll be right back," I told her. "I just had an idea."

I dashed down the alley to Mrs. Skilos' house. My idea (I did have a little help from my mother) was that if Mrs. Skilos got out more often and saw more people, it would be good for her.

When we got back to the alley picnic, I introduced her to everyone around the table.

"What lovely children you are!" she exclaimed.

"And you're a lovely child, too," Mr. Plouffe told her.

The two of them were made for each other.

Just then a police car came down the alley and stopped at our barricade, which was made of three plastic traffic cones set in a line. A policewoman got out of the car.

"Do you have a permit to occupy this alley?" she asked in a serious voice.

"Oh, look! That lady looks just like a policeman," Mrs. Skilos said loudly.

It was pretty hard not to laugh.

"We need a permit to have a picnic?" my mother asked.

"The alley is a public road. You're not allowed to

block it. What happens if a fire truck needs to get through here?"

We looked up and down the alley. The sun was setting, and all we could hear were birds. No fire trucks in sight.

"If a fire truck wants to get through, you can be sure we'll move our tables," my father told her.

"I love a man in a uniform," Mrs. Skilos added. "Don't you?"

The policewoman tried to look serious. But as she drove away, she honked her horn and waved.

"That's a relief," Mr. Plouffe said. "I thought we were all going to jail."

I think next year, my summer job will be taking care of Mr. Plouffe, too.

Just after the sun went down, we heard explosions in the distance.

"*Viva España!*" Flor's parents shouted.

"Tonight is the last night of the Montreal fireworks competition," Flor said. "And it's Spain's turn."

"Spain will win," her father said. "They won the World Cup. They're the best!"

Right on cue, there was a giant explosion of colored lights in the sky right over the Mountain — red and yellow, the colors of Spain. Flor's parents waved the little Spanish flags they'd brought with them.

"If you want Spain to win," I said to Flor, "then so do I."

It was a great end to my birthday, and a great end to summer, too. Summer in the city turned out to be full of adventures after all. In my neighborhood, I could find just about everything — even fireworks. And we didn't have to leave our alley to see them.

There was one more thing. Flor would be in my class in September...

THE END

Marie-Louise Gay is an author and illustrator of children's books. Her Stella and Sam books have been translated into more than fifteen languages. She has won many major awards, including two Governor General's awards, the Marilyn Baillie Picture Book Award and the Vicky Metcalf Award. She has been nominated twice for the Hans Christian Andersen Award.

Born and raised in Chicago, *David Homel* is an award-winning novelist, screenwriter, journalist and translator. He is a two-time winner of the Governor General's Award for translation and the author of six novels, including *The Speaking Cure* (winner of the Hugh MacLennan Prize and the Jewish Public Library Award for fiction) and, most recently, *Midway*.

Marie-Louise and David live in Montreal, but travel as much as possible.